THE
MASTER MYSTERY

Novelized by

ARTHUR B. REEVE
and JOHN W. GREY

From Scenarios by Arthur B. Reeve in Collaboration with
John W. Grey and C.A. Logue

1st WORLD
LIBRARY
Literary Society

The Master Mystery

Arthur B. Reeve and John W. Grey

© 1st World Library, 2007
PO Box 2211
Fairfield, IA 52556
www.1stworldlibrary.com
First Edition

LCCN: 2007923744

Softcover ISBN: 978-1-4218-4227-1
Hardcover ISBN: 978-1-4218-4129-8
eBook ISBN: 978-1-4218-4325-4

Purchase *"The Master Mystery"*
as a traditional bound book at:
www.1stWorldLibrary.com/purchase.asp?ISBN=978-1-4218-4227-1

1st World Library is a literary, educational organization
dedicated to:

- Creating a free internet library of downloadable ebooks

- Hosting writing competitions and offering book
publishing scholarships.

1ˢᵗ World Library Literary Society

Giving Back to the World

"If you want to work on the core problem, it's early school literacy."

- James Barksdale, former CEO of Netscape

"No skill is more crucial to the future of a child, or to a democratic and prosperous society, than literacy."

- Los Angeles Times

Literacy... means far more than learning how to read and write... The aim is to transmit... knowledge and promote social participation."

- UNESCO

"Literacy is not a luxury, it is a right and a responsibility. If our world is to meet the challenges of the twenty-first century we must harness the energy and creativity of all our citizens."

- President Bill Clinton

"Parents should be encouraged to read to their children, and teachers should be equipped with all available techniques for teaching literacy, so the varying needs and capacities of individual kids can be taken into account."

- Hugh Mackay

CHAPTER I

Peter Brent sat nervously smoking in the library of his great house, Brent Rock.

He was a man of about forty-five or-six—a typical, shrewd business man. Something, however, was evidently on his mind, for, though he tried to conceal it, he lacked the self-assurance that was habitually his before the world.

A scowl clouded his face as the door of the library was flung open and he heard voices in the hall. A tall, spare, long-haired man forced his way in, crushing his soft black hat in his hands.

"I *will* see Mr. Brent," insisted the new-comer, as he pushed past the butler. "Mr. Brent!" he cried, advancing with a wild light in his eyes. "I'm tired of excuses. I want justice regarding that water-motor of mine." He paused, then added, shaking his finger threateningly, "Put it on the market—or I will call in the Department of Justice!"

Brent scowled again. For years he had been amassing a fortune by a process that was scarcely within the law.

For, when inventions threaten to render useless already existing patents, necessitating the scrapping of millions of dollars' worth of machinery, vested interests must be protected.

Thus, Brent and his partner, Herbert Balcom, had evolved a simple method of protecting corporations against troublesome inventors and inventions. They had formed their own corporation, International Patents, Incorporated.

Their method was effective—though desperate. It was to suppress the inventor and his labor. They bought the sole rights from the inventor, promising him glittering royalties. The joker was that the invention was suppressed. None were ever manufactured. Hence there were no royalties and the corporations went on undisturbed while Brent and Balcom collected huge retainers for the protection they afforded them.

Thus Brent Rock had come to be hated by scores of inventors defrauded in this unequal conflict with big business.

The inventor looked about at the library, richly paneled in oak and luxuriously furnished. Through a pair of folding-doors he could see the dining-room and a conservatory beyond. All this had been paid for by himself and such as he.

"Sit down, sir," nodded Brent, suavely.

The man continued to stand, growing more and more excited. Had he been a keener observer he would have seen that under Brent's suavity there was a scarcely hidden nervousness.

Finally Brent leaned over and spoke in a whisper, looking about as though the very walls might have ears.

"My dear fellow," he confided, "for some time I have been considering your water-motor. I will return the model to you—release the patent to the world."

He drew back to watch the effect on the aged inventor. Could it be that Brent was lying? Or was it fear? Could it be that at last his seared conscience was troubling him?

At that exact moment, up-stairs, in a private laboratory in the house, sat a young man at a desk—a handsome, strong-faced, clean-cut chap. All about him were the scientific instruments which he used to test inventions offered to Brent.

A look of intent eagerness passed over his face. For Quentin Locke was not testing any of Brent's patents just now. Over his head he had the receivers of a dictagraph.

It was a strange act for one so recently employed as manager of Brent's private laboratory. Yet such a man must have had his reasons.

One who was interested might have followed the wire from the dictagraph-box in the top drawer of the desk down the leg of the desk, through the very walls to the huge chandelier in the library below, where, in the ornamented brass-work, reposed a small black disk about the size of a watch. It was the receiving-end of the dictagraph.

Suddenly the young man's face broke out into a smile and without thinking he stopped writing what the little mechanical eavesdropper was conveying him from below. He listened intently as he heard a silvery laugh over the wire.

"Oh, I didn't know you were busy. I thought these flowers—Well, never mind. I'll leave them, anyway."

It was Eva Brent, daughter of the head of the firm, who had danced in from the conservatory like a June zephyr in December.

"My dear," Locke could hear the patent magnate welcome, "it is all right. Stay a moment and talk to this gentleman while I go down to the museum."

Locke listened eagerly, glancing now and then at a photograph of Eva Brent on his own desk, while she chatted gaily with the inventor. It was evident that Eva had not the faintest idea of the hard nature of the business of her father.

Meanwhile, Brent himself had left the library and passed through the portiered door into the hall. He did not turn up the grand staircase in the center of the wide hall, but hurried, preoccupied, to a door under the stairs that opened down to the cellar.

He started to open it to pass down. As he did so he did not hear a light footstep on the stairs as his secretary, Zita Dane, came down. But he did not escape her watchful eye.

"Mr. Brent," she called, "is there anything I can do?"

Brent paused. "Wait a moment for me in the library," he directed, as he turned again to enter the cellar.

He closed the door and Zita watched him with an almost uncanny interest, then turned to the library to join Eva and the new-comer.

Down the cellar steps Brent made his way, and across the cellar floor, pausing at the rocky wall of the foundation of the house blasted and hewn out of the cliff on which it towered above the river. A heavy steel door in the rock wall barred the way.

Brent whirled the combination and shot the bolts, and the door swung ponderously open, disclosing a rock-hewn cavern. Three walls of the cavern were lined with shelves

Arthur B. Reeve and John W. Grey

containing inventions of all kinds—telegraph and telephone instruments, engine models, railroad-signaling and safety devices, racks of bottles containing dangerous chemicals and their antidotes—all conceivable manner of mechanical and scientific paraphernalia. It was literally a Graveyard of Genius—harboring the ghosts of a thousand inventors' dead hopes.

Brent entered hastily and went directly to a shelf. There he picked up a model of a motor. He blew the dust from it and examined it approvingly.

Suddenly he saw something that caused him to start. He looked down at his feet. There was a piece of paper on the floor.

He picked it up and read it, and as he did so he started back, frightened—then angry. He looked about at the rock-hewn cavern walls—then read again:

> BRENT—This is my last warning. If you persist in your course you will be struck down by the Madagascar madness.
>
> Q.

Under his breath, Brent swore. Again he looked about the cavern, then turned hurriedly, picked up the motor, passed out the steel door, clanged it shut, and locked it.

No sooner had Brent shut the door, however, than it seemed as if the very face of the outer rocky wall of the cavern began to move—to tilt, as if on hinges.

If a human eye had been in the Graveyard of Genius at that instant it would have sworn that it perceived in the inky blackness of the tilting rock a passage, and in the shadows of that passage a huge, weird, grotesque figure peering in.

Then the tilting rock door closed again, as the figure disappeared down the rocky passage on the opposite side—a menace and a threat to the owner of Brent Rock, insecure even in his millions.

CHAPTER II

When Brent arrived back at the library he had quite recovered his poise, at least to the eyes of those in the library. Zita had joined Eva with the old inventor, Davis.

As Brent entered, Davis uttered an exclamation of joy at the sight of his motor. For the moment Brent almost glowed.

"Along with your invention," he beamed, as he handed the model to the old man, "I am going to release many others to the world."

All this not only Locke was noting, but Zita, too, appeared to be an almost too interested listener.

The others were chatting when Zita heard a noise in the hall and hurried out. She was just in time to see a rather hard-visaged man, with cruel, penetrating eyes. It was Herbert Balcom, vice-president of the company.

Zita whispered to him a moment and Balcom's hard face grew harder.

"Go up-stairs—watch *him*," he ordered, passing down the hall.

Balcom entered the library just as Davis was about to leave, hugging close to him his brain child. Davis clutched it a bit closer at sight of the other partner.

A glance would have been sufficient to show that Brent was secretly afraid of his partner, Balcom, and that Balcom dominated him.

"Go to the gate with him, my dear," whispered Brent to his daughter, who was clinging to his arm, convinced of the goodness of her father, ignorant of the very basis on which the Brent and Balcom fortune rested.

Balcom's mouth tightened as he came closer to Brent, menacing, the moment they were alone.

"How long has this double crossing been going on?" sneered Balcom, jerking his head toward the door through which Eva had just gone with the inventor, and shoving his face close to Brent's.

"It's not double crossing, Balcom," Brent attempted to conciliate, "but—"

"No 'buts,'" interrupted Balcom, with deadly coldness. "Keep on, and you'll have the government down on us for violating the anti-trust law. What's the matter? Have you lost your nerve?"

As Balcom almost hissed the question, up in the laboratory Locke was now writing furiously in his note-book, when he was interrupted by a knock at the door. He whipped the dictagraph receiver off his head and jumped to his feet, hiding all traces of the dictagraph in the desk drawer. Then he moved over to the door, unlocked it, and flung it open.

"Oh, I hope I haven't interrupted you in any important experiment," apologized Zita, innocently enough.

"Nothing important," camouflaged Locke.

Though Locke did not seem to notice it, another would have seen that Zita cared a great deal for him.

"May I come in?" she asked, wheedling.

"Certainly. I am charmed, I assure you."

While Zita was gushingly effusive, Locke was correct and formally polite as he bowed his acquiescence. Zita felt it.

For a moment she stood looking at a half-finished experiment on the laboratory table, then finally she turned to Locke with a calculated impulsiveness.

"Why do you treat me so coldly," she asked, "when you know I admire your wonderful work?"

"Really, Miss Dane," he apologized, "I didn't mean to be rude."

Yet there was an air of constraint in his very tone.

"Do you know," she flashed, "I can't help feeling that you are so brilliant—you must be something more than you seem."

Locke suppressed a quick look of surprise. Was she trying to worm some secret from him? He masked his face cleverly.

"Indeed, you must be imagining things," he replied, quietly, turning and strolling toward the window of his laboratory.

The moment his back was turned Zita picked up the photograph of Eva on the desk. For a moment she stood glaring at it jealously.

Out of the window Locke smiled. For, down on the gravel path, walking slowly toward the gate to the Brent Rock grounds, he could see Eva and Davis.

The smile faded into a scowl. He had seen a young man enter the gate. It was Paul Balcom, son of Herbert Balcom, and Paul was engaged to Eva—thus giving Balcom a stronger hold over Brent.

Locke knew enough about Paul to dislike him thoroughly and to distrust him. Had Locke been able to see over the hedge he would have confirmed his suspicions. For Paul had actually driven up to Brent Rock in the runabout of as notorious a woman as could have been found in the night life of the city—one known as De Luxe Dora in the unsavory half-world in which both were leaders. Had his dictagraph been extended to the hedge he would have heard her voice rasp at Paul:

"Your father may make you pay attention to this girl, Paul, but remember—you had not better double cross me."

Paul's protestations of underworld fidelity, would have added to Locke's fury.

However, Locke had not seen or heard. Still, it was unbearable that this fellow Paul should be engaged to a girl like Eva. Tall, dark, handsome though he was, Locke knew him to be a man not to be trusted.

Paul hurried up to Eva, not a bit disconcerted at the near discovery of his intimacy with Dora. And, whatever one may believe about woman's intuition, there must have been something in it, for even at a distance one could see that Eva mistrusted Paul Balcom, her fiance. Locke scowled blackly.

Paul thrust himself almost rudely between Davis and Eva.

Arthur B. Reeve and John W. Grey

Again Davis shrank, as he had from the young man's father, then bowed, excused himself, and hurried off, hugging his motor to him, while Paul took Eva's hand, which she was not any too willing to give him. Locke watched, motionless, as the couple turned back to the house.

Somehow Eva must have felt his gaze. She turned and looked upward at the laboratory window. As she saw Locke her face broke into a smile and she waved her hand gaily. Paul saw it and a swift flush of anger crossed his face. He pulled Eva abruptly by the arm.

"Let's go into the house," he said, almost angrily.

Seeing the action, Locke also turned from the window to encounter Zita, still watching. Without a word he left the laboratory.

While this little quadrangle of conflicting emotions of Locke, Eva, Paul, and Zita was being enacted the two partners in the library were disputing hot and heavy. As they argued, almost it seemed as if Balcom's very face limned his thoughts—that he desired Brent out of the way, as a weakling in whom he had discovered some traces of cons-cience which, to Balcom, meant weakness.

Balcom leaned forward excitedly. "I do not intend to let you wreck this company because your conscience, as you call it, has begun to trouble you," he hissed.

Brent's hand clutched nervously. He was afraid of Balcom—so much so that he fought back only weakly.

Locke was down in the hallway just in time to meet Eva and Paul as they entered.

"Oh—do you know, I'm so glad—I think my father is the

most kind-hearted of men," Eva trilled to Locke, as she recounted what had happened in the library with Davis.

Locke listened with restrained admiration for the girl, whatever might have been his secret opinion of her father or of the story he already knew.

On his part, Paul did not relish the situation, nor did he take any pains to conceal it. He shrugged and turned away.

"Come," he said, with a tone of surly authority, "I think I hear my father in the library."

Eva looked back swiftly at Locke and smiled as Paul led her toward the library door. But that, also, made Paul more furious.

"Why do you make me ridiculous before that fellow?" he demanded.

"I'm sorry," replied Eva, in surprise. "I didn't meant to do that."

Vaguely Paul understood. The girl was too unsophisticated to have meant it. Somehow that made it worse. Though she did not know it, he did. Unknown to herself, there was a response in the presence of Locke which was not inspired in his own society. He hurried her into the library.

It was as though the entrance of Paul and Eva had been preconcerted. The partners, in their dispute, stopped and turned as the young people entered and moved over to a divan. Balcom lowered his voice and plucked at Brent's sleeve as he nodded toward the couple.

"I could trust you better if they were married within a week," suggested Balcom.

Brent recoiled, but Balcom affected not to notice.

"Then I will believe that you are dealing fairly with me," he emphasized.

Brent studied a moment, then nodded assent. Balcom extended a cold, commanding hand and the partners shook hands.

Outside, Locke had paused, about to enter the library. The pause had been just long enough for him to hear—and it was a blow to him. He watched, dazed, as the two older men walked over to the younger couple; then he turned away, heart sick.

"My dear," began Brent, as he patted the shoulder of the girl, the one spot of goodness that had shone in the otherwise blackness of his life, making him at last realize the depth to which lust of money had made him sink, "we were just saying that perhaps it would be advisable to—er—hasten your marriage to Paul—say—perhaps next week."

The words seemed to stick in his throat.

As for Eva, she felt a shiver pass over her. Without knowing why, she drew back from Paul, at her side, shrank even closer to her father, trying not to tremble. Did Paul realize it?

Brent felt the shudder with a pang. He leaned over. "Promise to do this—for my sake," he whispered, so low that there was no chance of the others hearing. "By to-morrow all may be changed."

There was something ominous about the very words.

CHAPTER III

Brent had no intention of keeping the promise which Balcom had extracted from him by a species of moral duress that afternoon.

In fact, already he had gone too far in his plans for restitution—or was it self-preservation?—to turn back. It was late in the night that he himself secretly admitted to the house a tall, dark-haired stranger who evidently called by appointment.

"Well, Flint," he greeted, in a hushed tone, "what was it you asked to see me about?"

Flint replied not a word, but impressively tapped a bundle which he carried under his arm and began to undo the cord which bound it.

Brent looked startled, then caught himself. He had known Flint for some time—an adventurer, more or less unscrupulous, who had been the foreign representative of International Patents.

Flint took off his coat and threw it on a chair with an air of assurance that seemed to increase Brent's anxiety, then began again to untie the bulky package.

"Just a moment, Flint," cautioned Brent, stopping him.

With an air of uneasy secrecy Brent hurried to the door that led from the dining-room to the conservatory and bolted it securely. Then he made sure that the door to the library was bolted.

As he did so he did not see his secretary, Zita, watching in the hall, for the footsteps of Locke, approaching, had caught her quick ear and she had fled.

"Locke!" called Brent, hearing his laboratory, manager. "Under no circumstances allow me to be disturbed to-night."

"Very well, sir," responded Locke.

Just then the light step of Eva was heard on the stairs.

"What's the matter, father?" she asked, still upset by the events of the afternoon. "Is there anything wrong?"

"No, my dear, nothing," hastily replied Brent. "In the morning I shall have something to say to you. Now run along like a good girl."

Dutifully Eva turned. Brent watched her out of sight. Then with a keen look at Locke he pulled out a paper from his pocket and handed it to the young scientist, who read:

> BRENT,—This is my last warning. If you persist in your course you will be struck down by the Madagascar madness.
>
> Q.

Locke looked up from the scrawl in alarmed perplexity.

"What does this mean?" he queried.

Brent merely shook his head cryptically.

"Study this message. I shall have something very important to tell you in the morning."

As Brent turned back into the library he paused a moment and looked after Locke, hesitating, as if he would call him back. Then he decided not to do so, turned, and carefully locked the door from the dining-room into the hallway.

Eva was waiting at the head of the stairs as Locke, perplexed by the strange actions of his employer, came up.

"What *is* the trouble?" she repeated, anxiously. "Please tell me. Is there anything wrong?"

"No—nothing," reassured Locke, in spite of his own doubt. "Everything is all right."

"I hope so." Eva lingered. "Good night."

Locke bowed admiringly. But there was the same restraint in his look that had been shown in the afternoon.

"Good night," he murmured, slowly.

Eva quite understood, and there was a smile of encouragement on her face as she turned away and flitted down the hall to her room.

Outside, Zita had hurried from the house to the nearest public telephone-booth and was frantically calling Balcom at his apartment.

"Mr. Balcom," she repeated, breathlessly, as the junior

partner answered, "Flint has returned. I have seen him."

"The devil!" exclaimed Balcom, angrily, then checked himself before he said any more. "Keep me informed."

Abruptly he hung up.

It was scarcely a moment later that Paul Balcom entered the Balcom apartment, admitted by a turbaned black suggestive of the Orient.

Paul was surly and had evidently been drinking, for he shoved the servant roughly out of the way as he strode toward his father.

Apparently outside Paul had overheard and had gathered the drift of what Balcom had been saying. Or perhaps, from his own sources of information, he already knew. At any rate, as Balcom turned from the telephone, father and son faced each other angrily.

"Brent's lying," exclaimed Paul. "That marriage to me must take place to-morrow."

Talking angrily, sometimes in agreement, at others far apart, the two left the room.

Back in the dining-room by this time Brent had rejoined Flint and now watched him eagerly as he took the last wrappings from the package which he had carried so carefully.

As the last wrapping was stripped from it, on the table before them lay a small steel model, perhaps three feet high —a weird-looking thing in the miniature shape of a man, designed along lines that only a cubist could have conceived —jointed, mobile, truly a contrivance at which to marvel.

Brent gazed incredulously at the strange thing. "An auto-maton!" he exclaimed.

"More than that," replied Flint, calmly.

Flint unrolled a chart of the human nervous system and spread it out on the table. Pointing to the brain, he leaned over tensely, and whispered:

"This model is merely a piece of mechanism. But the real automaton possesses a human brain which has been transplanted into it and made to guide it."

For a moment Brent listened incredulously, then sat back in his chair and laughed skeptically. But even Flint recognized that there was a hollowness in the laughter.

"Do you mean to tell me," demanded Brent, "that a human brain has been made to control a thing of no use except as a terrible engine of destruction?"

"Not only possible," reiterated Flint, "but it is true."

"Oh, Flint," rallied Brent, with a sort of uneasiness, "you can't tell *me* that!"

"Believe it or not," insisted the adventurer, "I have been in Madagascar and I know."

For a moment Brent paused at the vehemence of Flint's answer. What had Flint to gain by misrepresentation? A thousand images of the past flitted through Brent's brain. Then slowly a look of terror came over Brent's face. Suppose it were indeed true—this Frankenstein, this conscienceless inhuman superman? Brent gripped himself and composed his features and his voice.

"But this thing," he rasped. "What does this prove?"

"Oh, this is merely automatic—a piece of mechanism—a model which I stole. It works when it is wound up—not like the real one. Look."

Flint put a pencil in the little steel hand of the model and pressed a lever as he held a piece of paper under the pencil. Brent leaned over, fascinated.

Instantly the tiny hand began to trace on the paper one letter—the simple letter "Q."

As the hand finished the tail of the "Q" Brent gripped the table for support. His eyes bulged and stared wildly.

"My God!" burst from his lips. "It is the warning—Q!"

For minutes Brent strove to regain his composure.

Nor was Flint less impressed than the man before him.

What would have been the emotions of both if they had been able to penetrate with the eye through the rocky cliffs on which the stately mansion of Brent Rock stood would have been hard to say.

For, down in a rock-hewn cavern, not many hundred yards away and below them, reached by a secret entrance from the shrubbery of the cliffs near the shore, already had congregated several rough characters. They were playing cards and drinking, now and then glancing furtively at the passage entrance, as though they were expecting the arrival of some one or something.

Suddenly came a dull metallic clank through the passage, strangely echoing. At once all leaped to their feet, at attention, not unmixed with awe and fear that sat strangely on their desperate features. What was it that they, who feared neither God nor man, feared?

They strained their eyes, looking into the passage that led darkly away into blackness.

Dimly down it now could be seen two gleaming spots of light, points in the Cimmerian darkness. They seemed to be growing larger and coming nearer as with each hollow reverberation the dull metallic thuds increased.

Faintly now could be made out in the blackness a huge, stalking figure, having the shape of a man, with gigantic, powerful shoulders, powerful arms, a thick body, hips, and thighs that spelled terrific strength, legs and feet that suggested irresistible force.

"The Automaton!" escaped involuntarily from all lips.

Slowly, irresistibly, the horrendous figure stalked forth into the dim light. There it paused for a moment—a figure of steel, larger than most men, yet not so large but that it might have incased a man. And yet its motions, its every action, were like nothing mortal. Even these hardened denizens of the underworld shuddered.

In its hand the Automaton carried a five-branched candle-stick, for what purpose none seemed to know. Yet all bowed and quaked at every pantomime motion of the figure, ready to do the bidding of the least motion of their inhuman master.

Still holding the candlestick with its five huge yellow candles before him, the Automaton stalked forward to the table and impressively deposited the candlestick on it, then stepped back a pace and waved his ponderous hand at the assembled emissaries, who scarcely repressed their own abject terror.

CHAPTER IV

At a motion from the Automaton a dark-skinned Madagascan stepped forward and lighted the five candles. At once a dense smoke began drifting from the candles.

The men looked at one another, showing an uncomfortable fear of what the negro and the Automaton were doing. Even the negro edged away fearfully and all crouched back, afraid of the fumes.

A moment later the Automaton, with a mighty blast of air, snuffed all the candles at once, then, without a word, picked up the candlestick and stalked off through the passage on the opposite side of the den from the entrance, the passage that led to the Graveyard of Genius.

A few moments later the secret rock door from this passage into the Graveyard swung open and the Automaton stalked in, going carefully, noiselessly, now. Across the floor he walked to the steel door, which he swung open, then on out into the cellar of Brent Rock and up the steps to the door under the stairs that led to the hallway of the great house.

In the hall the Automaton halted beside a small stand on which stood a candlestick exactly like the one he carried. Quickly he picked up the original candlestick and replaced it by the one he carried. Then he set the original back of the portieres, and with a glance at the library door turned back to the cellar, closing the door noiselessly behind him.

Down the steps he went, toward the open door of the Graveyard of Genius. Beside the door was the fuse-box of the lighting system of the house.

The Automaton reached out and began rubbing sharply at the insulation of the feed wires.

Up-stairs, in the dining-room, Brent had by this time flung off his coat and was examining with Flint the curious model the adventurer had brought from Madagascar. Brent was very excited and questioned Flint eagerly.

"I tell you, Flint," cried Brent, at length, huskily, as he seized a pen and dipped in into the ink, "the time has come for me to do what I have long intended. I am going to do now what I should have done years ago."

Brent started to write feverishly:

QUENTIN LOCKE,—I have done you a great injury about which you know nothing, but I am willing to—

His hand had scarcely traced the last word when the room was plunged into absolute darkness.

Down in the cellar the Automaton had succeeded in rubbing off the insulation of the feed wires. There was a flash of light as he laid his steel hand over the two feed wires —then darkness.

In the dining-room Brent and Flint, already keyed to the highest pitch, leaped to their feet with an exclamation of terror.

Late as it was, Locke was working in his laboratory on the

second floor of the house when the lights winked out. Surprised for the moment, he ran out into the hall.

Already there was the butler, groping about with a candle.

"What's the matter, Quentin?" asked a breathless voice behind them.

It was Eva in a filmy dressing-gown. Locke turned to vision a creation of loveliness in the candle-light which set his heart thumping.

"Nothing," he reassured. "Just the lights short-circuited, that's all. I'll see."

Just then the dining-room door opened and Eva saw her father, disheveled and preoccupied, stride out and take the five-branched candlestick from the hall table. Nervously he began to light the candles. They sputtered a bit and he turned quickly, still holding the candlestick, as the smoke drifted away from them all.

"Fix the fuses in the cellar," he directed the butler.

"Is anything—really the matter—father?" implored Eva.

"No, no, my child," he answered, hastily. "Go back to bed. And, Locke, please don't let us be disturbed."

He was about to say more, then decided not to do so, and turned back into the dining-room.

Again Brent carefully locked the door to the dining-room and rejoined Flint.

He had placed the candles on the table, not noticing in the half-light that the smoke from them was growing denser as they burned down.

The smoke drifted over as the draught carried it. Flint coughed and moved a bit, his hand at his throat.

Brent seized the pen again and was about to write, when the smoke from the candles drifted into his own face. He, too, coughed.

Uneasy, Brent glanced over at Flint. Flint laughed, a bit hysterically.

"What the devil's the matter?" demanded Brent, with lowered brows, a strange dryness in his throat.

Flint was now leaning forward on his elbows and laughing foolishly, stupidly. It was a queer laugh, and struck terror into Brent as he himself coughed and clutched involuntarily at his throat. Brent stared at Flint.

"What is it?" he repeated, anxiously. "Have you suddenly gone mad, man?"

But there was no reply. Instead, Flint laughed all the more madly.

Brent was more than startled. If he could have seen himself in a glass he would have seen that he was already wide-mouthed and disheveled. Suddenly the smoke again blew in his face. He coughed again. His head reeled.

Then, in a flash, it all dawned on him.

He shielded himself from the candles. But it was too late.

"My God!" he exclaimed, starting up. "The Madagascar madness!"

Brent looked about wildly. He rushed to Flint and shook him. But Flint only laughed. He turned and moved toward the candles, reaching out for them. But even as he did so his hand faltered.

He stopped and passed his hand across his tightening forehead. Slowly over his face came a stupid expression. He felt himself going, without power of retraining himself. His lips twitched and he swayed.

Then he began to laugh uncontrollably.

Flint rose and clapped him on the shoulder. Then both laughed foolishly, loudly.

They were beyond help. It was the laughing madness.

Outside, in the hall, Eva and Locke had been standing, talking for a moment, when suddenly, below, they heard a terrific noise in the cellar. Involuntarily Eva's hand clutched Locke's arm. Locke drew a revolver and, in spite of Eva's fearsome caution, hastened down the cellar stairs.

About in the blackness of the cellar he groped until his foot touched something soft, a mass on the floor. He bent over. It was the butler, in a heap, unconscious, but still breathing.

There was not a sound, not another being in the cellar.

Together Eva and Locke helped the now half-conscious man to his feet and pushed and pulled him up the stairs; as slowly he recovered his power of speech.

"What was it—tell us?" urged Locke.

"I—I went down to fix the fuses—as the master ordered," muttered the butler, incoherently. "A huge figure—steel hand—it flung me across the floor—the last I remember."

He passed his hand over his head as though recollection even was too horrible for description.

Locke listened a bit doubtfully, then sent the butler on his way to bed, while Eva could scarcely restrain her fears.

Over to the dining-room door Locke strode and listened. There was nothing but the sound of merriment inside, of uncontrollable laughter. Could it be that Brent and Flint were drinking? He dared not betray a fear to Eva. Instead he knocked.

At that moment he could hear the sound of some heavy body falling; then more laughter as Brent in his hysteria struck the model of the automaton to the floor.

With the model, unnoticed by Brent, now fluttered to the floor the letter he had been writing. But the madman paid no attention to that now as it sifted through the air and fluttered under the sideboard.

"Mr. Brent," called Locke, "please open the door."

Instead of an answer came a loud and insulting laugh, followed by an incoherent mouthing of words. Eva looked startled, blanched. It was so unlike her father. For the moment Locke was piqued. But he tried not to show it as he turned away from the door.

"I am your father's employe," he said, sadly, "and it is his privilege, I suppose, to laugh at me." He hesitated.

"Oh, but, Quentin—Mr. Locke—I'm—I'm so sorry. Surely he could not have meant it."

At the head of the stairs Locke tried to smile.

"Don't worry," he said, repressing his feelings. "It will make no difference between us. Good night."

They parted, Eva closing her door for a sleepless night, Locke to work far into the night in his laboratory until sheer exhaustion overcame his feelings.

Meanwhile, in the dining-room, the two men kept terrible vigil, hour after hour, oblivious of time, in wild and wanton laughter—maniacal abandon.

A terrible blow had been struck and Reason was tottering on her throne.

Two men had been stricken by an unknown hand—stark, stark mad.

CHAPTER V

"Father—please—open the door!"

It was early the following morning that the butler with frightened face had called Eva Brent to tell her that her father and Flint had been locked in the dining-room all night and were still laughing madly.

Eva had hurried down-stairs, encountering Zita as she ran. It was true. She could hear the voices inside. Nor could she get any answer from the two men.

"Oh—Zita—please—can't something be *done?*" Eva implored.

With a hasty word Zita hurried away just as Herbert Balcom himself entered the house from the street.

In utter surprise Balcom nodded at Zita as she poured forth the story of what had been discovered in the morning, then pushed past her in high excitement.

"What's wrong?" he asked as he came upon the butler and Eva still knocking excitedly at the dining-room door.

Eva was almost in a panic as she answered, "Father and Mr. Flint have been in there laughing ever since last night."

Arthur B. Reeve and John W. Grey

Balcom tried to comfort her. But somehow his sympathy sent a cold shudder through the poor girl.

Meanwhile Zita had encountered Locke hurrying down at the sound of the commotion. To him she told the story, again hurt that his interest was solely for Eva, not in herself.

Locke paused long enough to seize an umbrella from the rack, rip the cover off, and break out a rib, to which he tied a piece of string while he hurried to the group at the door.

"Break down the door and call the police," ordered Balcom.

The butler reached for a chair and was about to swing it over his head to break down the door.

"Stop!" interrupted Locke.

The young scientist knelt down, inserted the umbrella steel through the keyhole, and bent it by the string as he fished about with it on the other side to find the bolt. Meanwhile the butler telephoned frantically for the police.

It was at this height of excitement that Paul Balcom entered. A moment's talk with Zita, and he, too, joined the group.

Sympathetically he spoke to Eva, but Eva scarcely responded in the fashion of a girl to the man whom she was going to marry. Her attention was riveted on Locke, who was kneeling before the door. Paul saw it and an ominous scowl crossed his face.

Carefully Locke worked the umbrella steel and the string until he had caught the bolt. Then he shot the bolt back and rose to his feet. All watched him expectantly as he threw open the door.

Such a sight as met their eyes one could scarcely picture.

There were Brent and Flint at the table—laughing—laughing. The candles had long since burned out. On the floor lay the automaton model.

"Father!" cried Eva, running to him.

But there was no look of recognition on Brent's face.

"Don't you know me? Speak to me! Father!"

Instead, Brent merely patted her shoulder and laughed hollowly. Eva, on her knees by him, sobbed and smoothed his head by turns.

Locke, bending over Flint, found him in much the same condition.

Meanwhile, Balcom and Paul had picked up the model of the automaton and exchanged a quick glance.

"This man Locke's actions are suspicious," exclaimed Balcom, hastily. "He was in the house last night."

Outside they could hear the arrival of the detectives summoned by the butler.

"Go to Eva," nudged Balcom to Paul.

A moment later the butler entered with the detectives.

At the sight of the automaton model in Balcom's hands the butler cried out:

"That is what attacked me last night—only larger—much larger!"

All eyes were now on the butler. Quickly Balcom took advantage of the situation thus created. Locke, also, left Flint and moved over to the group examining the model. As he did so his eye caught a piece of paper under the sideboard. He was about to pick it up when he realized that all were looking at him. Quickly he covered his discovery and faced them.

"This man is the stranger in the house," cried Balcom, in anger. "Arrest him and make him explain."

It was the work of only an instant for the chief detective to step up to Locke and slip the bracelets on his wrists.

"Don't!" cried Eva.

"Please—my dear—your father," remonstrated Paul.

At that instant Brent was seized with another violent fit of coughing and laughter. Eva, distracted, was half fainting.

Thus, with Locke handcuffed, Balcom and Paul were triumphant.

Locke saw his chance. But the handcuffs prevented him from using his hands. In the instant that all were diverted toward Brent, with incredible deftness Locke slipped his hand from the cuffs, one link of which fell open as if by magic, through a secret all his own. He reached down and picked up the paper under the sideboard and read it. It was the letter Brent had been writing and served only to increase his perplexity. He read it again, then crushed it into his pocket, and before any one had discovered his trick had slipped his hand back into the cuffs and they were locked again.

At that very moment the telephone rang and the chief of the

detectives answered. As he did so a perplexed expression crossed his face and he walked over quickly to Locke.

"I—beg your pardon," he apologized as he began to unlock the handcuffs.

"Here, my man, what are you doing?" interrupted Balcom.

"I know my business. You lay off," growled the detective.

A moment later Locke, with a slight smile on his handsome face, was answering the telephone.

Not a soul save the detective, even yet, suspected the true identity of Locke, even as he answered over the telephone with a respectful, "Yes, sir."

The fact of the matter was that the message had come most opportunely. It was from the chief of the Department of Justice himself, ordering Locke to stay at the house until he had secured the evidence that would allow the department to proceed against the company under the anti-trust law. That, then, was the explanation of the secret dictagraph which Locke had installed, the explanation of his apparent faithlessness to his employer.

But weightier matters were now on Locke's mind. Here he was faced by the case of his life, involving the happiness of the very girl whom he had so soon come to love. His incentive was double—love and success: triple—above all, justice.

By this time the household themselves were sufficiently calm to help Brent to his bedroom and Flint to a guest-chamber.

Balcom was about to follow, when Locke, returning from the telephone, touched him on the shoulder and shoved the threat message which Brent had given him the night before under the face of the junior partner.

"Read that," he demanded.

Balcom read, controlling his features admirably, if control were necessary.

"What's the meaning of this?" he demanded, coldly.

"Were you in Madagascar lately?" shot back Locke.

Locke could not be sure whether or not Balcom suppressed a start. At any rate, he did not conceal anger at the insinuation.

"Certainly," he replied. "With my son I cruised through the Mozambique Channel and touched at Madagascar last summer. Why?"

Locke nodded and the detective made a note of the reply.

"What do you mean to insinuate by that question?" demanded Balcom.

Without reply Locke shrugged nonchalantly and smiled.

Not ten feet away, in the conservatory door, Paul listened, and his face darkened as he clenched his fists.

There was a murderous glare in Paul's eyes as Locke unconcernedly withdrew, whispering to the detective, who nodded deferentially to the young scientist who had been assigned by the Department of Justice, strangely, to the very case which now he realized in some unknown way must concern himself and the very mystery of his own identity.

So wore along the morning, with growing mystery and excitement.

It was not long before the Brent family physician was summoned, and after a careful diagnosis pronounced Brent in a hopeless state as far as his own science was concerned. Eva was by this time more than frantic. The consolation of Paul seemed to add to her nervousness. She was almost distracted when she heard Balcom and the doctor discussing the case in low tones in her father's room.

"Don't you think, Doctor," she overheard, "that he would be far better off in a sanitarium?"

She shuddered as the doctor agreed with Balcom, and Balcom sought to persuade her that the course was best. Even the solicitations of Paul annoyed her. Paul was more than vexed at this new repulse from his bride-to-be. His anger knew no bounds as he caught sight of Locke, who had overheard and showed his doubt over the whole proposal for the care of Brent. He plucked at his father's sleeve and nodded toward Locke.

Balcom needed no prompting from his crafty son.

"I'll have you understand, Locke," he cried, his face growing apoplectic red, "that I am in charge here now. Your services are no longer required."

"I quite understand," returned Locke, quietly. "We shall see."

Balcom stormed down from the room to the telephone, where, a moment later, he telephoned to an asylum, asking them to send a conveyance with nurses, keepers, and whatever paraphernalia was necessary to take care of his partner, Brent.

Arthur B. Reeve and John W. Grey

"Is he violent?" demanded the doctor over the telephone.

"Yes. Bring a strait-jacket," snapped back Balcom. "And the sooner he is under your care the better."

With that Balcom stamped out of the house.

In Brent's room, Paul was attempting still to ingratiate himself with Eva, who was growing more distant toward him with every moment. Finally Paul could stand it no longer. He turned on his heel and faced Locke angrily in the hall.

"You'll regret this, confound you!" he ground out, as he swung out of the room rapidly in a high state of feeling.

Unconcernedly Locke turned on his heel.

"Don't worry," he whispered to Eva. "I'll see that no harm comes to your father."

For answer, her own heart too full for words, Eva pressed the hand of the young scientist. It was reward enough for Locke.

Meanwhile, at Doctor Shaw's sanitarium, to which Balcom had telephoned with the permission of the doctor, elaborate preparations had been completed for the reception and transportation of Brent.

It was perhaps an hour later that the ambulance, with three white-uniformed attendants, pulled out, carrying all those appurtenances necessary for the care of the insane, including the strait-jacket which Balcom had so testily suggested.

That same hour had seen intense activity in another quarter. In the den of the Automaton, the hard-visaged emissaries had been already roused by the entrance of the Automaton.

Hasty directions had been uttered by the metallic, phonograph voice of the monster, and already four of the most desperate of the characters had hurried through the entrance out on the cliffs. The Automaton himself had turned toward the passage through the Graveyard of Genius to Brent Rock itself.

Thus it happened that when the ambulance from Doctor Shaw's sanitarium came bowling along the road to Brent Rock as fast as its motor would permit, the driver was forced suddenly to put on the brakes to save himself from being wrecked by a huge log that lay squarely across the road.

No sooner had the attendants jumped out to remove the log than four desperate men fell upon them from ambush, beat them, and left them trussed up and unconscious, while they donned the jackets and uniforms of Doctor Shaw's men, seized the ambulance, and swung off again at a fast clip in the direction of Brent Rock.

Lulled into a false security, as her father slept now for a time under an opiate, Eva was sitting beside him with loving care when she heard the noise below of the arrival of the car from Doctor Shaw's sanitarium. At once she was in wild alarm. Nor was Locke off his guard. While Zita tried to reassure Eva, Locke met the men.

There were four of them, and as the first passed, Locke halted him. The parley gave another a chance to push past, while Locke held three at bay.

A moment later there was a scream from Eva, who had hurried from her father's room at the sound of the high voices. The emissary had seized her.

Arthur B. Reeve and John W. Grey

It was a signal for the other three, who leaped on Locke all at once. With almost superhuman strength Locke seized one of them and flung him over his head for a fall down the whole flight of steps as he fought the other two single-handed.

Even then the third came back to the attack and Locke was forced to give back step by step down the stairs.

Another scream from Eva.

In the heat of the fray Locke caught a glimpse of her battling on the landing above with the first emissary. It gave him redoubled strength.

Flinging the two men off and eluding the third, he leaped to the chandelier in the hall and with a giant swing wrapped his legs about the fellow struggling with Eva. Literally throttling him, he pulled him backward over the balcony railing for a fall clear to the lower hall.

At the moment when Locke was actually subduing all of his assailants the door to the cellar suddenly opened and the huge figure of the Automaton strode out.

With one blow of his steel fist the monster struck Locke senseless, then turned and began ascending the grand staircase.

Almost paralyzed with fear, Eva screamed again and fled through the nearest door, locking it. On strode the Automaton, crashing down the door as if it had been a mere shell.

Meanwhile the emissaries had seized Locke, still unconscious and unable to resist. Feverishly they began to bind him in the strait-jacket which they had taken from the ambulance. Then they carried him and flung him roughly on the floor of the library.

Still screaming, Eva fled to the next room, again bolting the door and piling furniture frantically to barricade it. Again the Automaton rained blow after blow on the door. It splintered, and his powerful fist began breaking and over-turning the barricade which the unfortunate girl had improvised.

Wildly she looked about. Only a closet now offered refuge. The door was splintered through. She could see the terrible face of the monster.

In the library, Locke, recovering by this time, began flopping and twisting, spurred by the muffled screams from above-stairs as he worked with miraculous dexterity to release himself from the strait-jacket.

CHAPTER VI

Locke struggled with superhuman effort to release himself from the strait-jacket in which he was held prisoner. The throat-straps pressed against the neck muscles and the strain on the straps could be heard like pistol-shots as the leather stretched under his prodigous efforts.

With every nerve keyed up and his reflexes answering his keen brain, he swayed backward and forward, rolled from side to side until his shoulder-blades were thrown completely out of joint. The pain was intense, but he summoned every ounce of strength at his command and finally succeeded in getting one of his arms free by gradually working his body toward a settee, where, with his elbow on the seat, he pushed his disjointed arm over his head.

Agony was written all over his face as at last with a final effort he extricated his arms and was in a position to loosen the straps which bound them, with his teeth.

Nor was his labor over now. The canvas jacket cut into his flesh and the buckles bruised his muscles. His body ached with weariness, yet he clung to his task. Like a thing incarnate he toiled as he realized the danger that confronted Eva.

Up-stairs, the monster was pursuing Eva. The heavy oaken

doors were as straws to him, and he plunged through them as a mad elephant dashes through a canebrake. Destruction lay in his wake as he crashed through the improvised barriers which Eva had constructed to delay his onslaught. A crouching, desolate figure, she waited for what she knew to be her end. There was only one barrier left between her and this engine of destruction. It was only a moment now when she would be a crushed, mangled mass. With terror in her heart she waited for the thing to crash through the last remaining barrier, and even now she could hear his ponderous step as he crossed the room toward the door which would only momentarily stay his progress. Her lips moved in prayer as she waited and the dread moments seemed eons to her.

Suddenly she heard a crash, and she could see the panels of sturdy oak in the door give way as though they were eggshells. The gigantic fist of the monster crashed through and she could discern the dim outline of the enormous head, and the glaring eyes of fire looking toward her. With a shrill shriek she raised her arms above her head and fell swooning to the floor just as a pistol-shot rang out.

Locke, disheveled and weak, had released himself from the strait-jacket, and with the speed of a panther had ascended the stairs. He saw the monster crashing through the last remaining barrier, and without hesitation he fired at the thing as he closed in. His one thought was to delay it or make it swerve in its course momentarily, with the hope that by some chance Eva might have time to escape. Could he only accomplish this, he thought his mission successful, regardless of the outcome as far as he himself was concerned.

He pulled the trigger of his automatic again and again as he rushed forward. By some strange trick of fate the figure reeled for a second and one of its arms dropped swinging to its side. The bullet had entered a joint. Had it in some way deranged the mechanism, causing the Automaton to turn in its tracks and confront Locke as he charged forward? Or was some human being concealed in the armored creature and wounded?

Eva, in her semi-conscious state, saw the mass of metal charge toward Locke, and closed her eyes so as not to be a witness to his end. She waited, dumb and helpless with fright, and before her surged the meaning of this man's great sacrifice for her. In the brief interval she realized that men of his ilk were few. She realized that her interest in the young chemist was more than a passing fancy and the truth was driven home to her in his hour of peril. She closed her eyes and all before her went blank.

As the Automaton faced Locke voices could be heard in the hall, and the gardener of Brent Rock, who had summoned aid, came to Locke's assistance. Armed with clubs and garden tools, the men charged the monster. Like a lion at bay, the thing turned from its task of destroying Locke to face its new enemies. *En masse* they attacked the Automaton, but it shook them off, one by one, as a terrier would rats, and made its way toward the grand staircase. Some of the gardener's aids suffered broken bones, while others were left unconscious as a result of the conflict.

Locke picked himself up and rushed to Eva's side. He took the prostrate form in his arms and looked down into her beautiful face. The room was in ruins, and Eva slowly opened her eyes and looked up at him. Her hand went out in a momentary caress, but as she fully recovered consciousness she moved her hand away lest he really know. She looked up at him gratefully, and Locke, a little confused, took his arm from around her waist. With boyish bashfulness he hung his head and asked her if she was all right. The sound of his own voice amid the ruins brought back his composure.

"We must see about father. Perhaps something has happened to him," said Eva, as she started toward the door.

Locke looked after the girl, then followed her.

Propped up in bed, Peter Brent presented a pitiable sight. His glassy stare and shrill laugh like a coyote baying at the moon sent cold chills down Eva's back as she entered the room. This man, at one time a power in the business world, was only a shell of his former self, and his inhuman laughter caused even Locke to shudder a little as he entered the room.

Eva walked over to her father and put her hand to his brow, looking wistfully in his eyes for some sign of recognition.

She kissed him on the forehead and called him, but he still stared blankly ahead of him, unconscious of even her presence. Locke felt the pulse of the patient and looked at the dilated pupils.

"There must be some antidote for this Madagascar madness, and I shall move everything to find it," he said, as he looked at Eva with determination.

She turned toward him eagerly as he spoke and his words gave her a little cheer. Eva continued her caresses, but the demented man showed no signs of recognizing even his own daughter.

From another room the shrill laughter of Flint could be heard as he raved in delirium. Bereft of reason, he fought an unseen enemy.

"Q did it, I tell you—it's Q," he raved and shrieked in his insane way as he rocked back and forth in bed. He was fighting his own conscience, and kept pushing some unseen thing from him as he shook in a paroxysm of fright.

The front-door bell rang and Balcom entered. He was suave in manner, but this time he seemed a little excited as he gave his hat and stick to the butler.

"Tell Miss Brent I must see her at once," he ordered.

As the butler turned to mount the stairs, Balcom reached his hand up and rubbed his shoulder as though he were in pain. Perhaps the gesture meant nothing, but a keen observer would have noticed that his arm did not move with the freedom that one would expect of a man of his frame and build. As he rubbed his shoulder his eyes followed the butler up the stairs and his lips tightened. He watched him until he was out of sight, then turned and entered the library.

As Balcom entered the library the door-bell rang and the three ambulance men who had been overpowered by the emissaries of the Automaton entered. Balcom approached them and hasty explanations were forthcoming. In his suave manner he quieted the most noisy of the trio, who by this time had found the strait-jacket from which Locke had just released himself.

"This looks like a put-up job to me," growled the driver, as he confronted Balcom, holding the strait-jacket toward him. "And I believe you know something about it."

"My dear man, I am the person who telephoned for you to come for my stricken partner," said Balcom, "and I still insist that he is in dire need of treatment."

As he spoke Eva entered the library in time to hear him. She was followed by Locke.

"My father shall not be taken from this house," she cried, in reply to Balcom's orders to the attendants.

As she spoke she turned toward Locke and looked at him for his acquiescence. He quietly nodded toward her in an assuring manner, and as he did so one might have noticed Balcom's face cloud up with evil purpose. He was thinking of this young whipper-snapper and his interference with his plans. As he stood meditating he noticed that Locke was looking at him, so he turned toward the young chemist and his whole expression changed. A bland smile crept across his face as he spoke.

"I was only suggesting that my partner be taken to an institution, because I believed that he would receive better treatment there." He addressed Locke, but looked toward Eva as he did so. "Miss Brent should have trust in me. I have only her interest at heart."

"It would be better for Mr. Brent to stay here," said Locke. "The treatment his daughter can give will be better than that of an outsider."

As he spoke he sauntered away with an air of finality, while Balcom shrugged his shoulders and gave orders to the ambulance men to go.

Locke walked toward the dining-room, and there amid the candle drippings and the wreckage of the night before espied the miniature automaton. He picked it up and examined it minutely as Balcom strolled in.

Balcom's quick gaze caught what Locke was looking at, and he approached the young chemist and sauvely said:

"It seems almost unbelievable, Mr. Locke, that a giant form like that could be endowed with a human brain."

As he spoke he pointed toward the miniature automaton in Locke's hands. Locke turned and faced him, his jaw tightening with a snap.

"Not unbelievable, but impossible, Mr. Balcom," he said. "I believe that there is some one in this thing that attacks us and calls himself Q."

He eyed Balcom as he spoke, to see the effects of his words. But if Balcom knew anything, he cunningly concealed it. Locke walked to the table and closely examined the candles and other stuff strewn about. He was looking for some clue to what had caused the madness of Brent and Flint. The crumpled anatomy chart lay on the floor, and as Locke stooped to pick it up Eva entered and came toward him. She shuddered slightly as she passed the miniature of the monster, and Balcom, with an air of satisfaction, noticed her fear. He turned and was about to go out, when the butler entered with the duplicate candlestick in his hands.

"Mr. Locke, in cleaning the hall I found this behind the portieres at the entrance to below-stairs," he announced. "I was quite puzzled for a moment, for I knew the master had taken it into the dining-room with him last evening."

As he spoke he handed the candlestick to Locke, who quickly compared it with the one on the dining-room table which contained the burnt candles.

In appearance the candelabra were identical. Locke with great care examined every feature of them, looking for a clue. He took one of the whole candles from the candlestick which the butler had brought in and scraped the wax from in with his penknife. He examined the particles carefully, then approached the candlestick which stood on the table the fatal night, and very carefully removed the wax from the stumps of candles which were still in the sockets.

"The Madagascar madness came from *that* candlestick," he announced, with assurance, as he pointed toward the one on the table.

While he was so busily engaged Balcom was eying him cunningly. He watched his every move and was most intent in seeing just how the young man would prove his contention.

"Good morning, every one!" came the clear voice of Paul as he entered the room and crossed over to the side of his fiancee. He was particular to ignore Locke in his greeting, and as he approached Eva he bent over her hand and kissed it.

A close observer would have noticed that the girl rather drew her hand back from his caress.

"I am so sorry about your father, Eva," whispered Paul. "I trust the ailment is but temporary."

As he spoke Eva thanked him mechanically for his solicitations, while Balcom glanced at his son in admiration.

Locke, who was still engaged in looking at the candle drippings through his pocket magnifying-glass, paid slight attention to Paul, but glanced up in time to see that there was a look of insincerity on his face.

Could it be that this young scion of the Balcom fortune could in any way be connected with the Automaton? Could this man, this suave, polished gentleman, have any motive for seeking the ruin or death of his fiancee? Locke seemed to be busily engaged in his task, but he was making mental notes on the conduct of young Balcom. He looked up finally and turned to Eva.

Arthur B. Reeve and John W. Grey

"Miss Brent, I find minute particles of some foreign substance in the wax of these candles," he announced. "They seem to be of organic origin and I am certain that they contain the poison which has robbed your father of his mentality. I am going to take them to a chemical laboratory where there will be proper facilities to have them analyzed. Perhaps there is an antidote that will restore your father's sanity."

As Locke spoke he carefully wrapped up the particles of drippings in a piece of paper and put them in his pocket. As he did so, both Balcom and Paul exchanged hurried glances, and Balcom left the group and started toward the hall.

During all this procedure Zita, clad in a sumptuous morning frock hardly befitting a secretary, was standing behind the portieres in the hall and listening intently to all she could hear within the dining-room. As she heard Balcom's footsteps she hurriedly turned and seemed to be going up the hall. He looked after her and then called.

She came toward Balcom with a nod of understanding, and, as she approached, he led her to a corner of the hall and whispered to her.

"It is imperative that we get Flint out of the house to-night. I can trust you to take care of this if I arrange the details?"

Zita quickly nodded acquiescence, looking furtively over her shoulder to see if they were observed.

"I will get him to your apartment," she hurriedly said, as she looked up at him for further instructions.

Balcom turned quickly from her, got his own hat and sack, and departed, just as Locke came into the hall, bound for the chemist's shop. He looked after the disappearing form of

Balcom, and then turned and noticed that he was being watched by Zita. Zita in turn hastily entered the library, without looking over her shoulder.

"I wonder what her real position in this house can be," mused Locke, as he took his hat and went toward the front door.

In the dining-room Paul was now standing close to Eva and had taken her hand.

"You know it was your father's wish that we be married," he was saying, "and I know that he would be happy if we had the ceremony performed at once."

His eyes narrowed as he said this, but Eva was too preoccupied to see it. With a shudder, ever so slight, she looked up at his handsome face and spoke.

"I will not even speak of marriage until my father recovers, Paul, and I don't know how you can ask me to at such a time."

She was not thinking so much of her father as of a certain young chemist who had risked his life for her. Why had fate thrown him in her way, she wondered. What was there about Quentin Locke that compelled her attention—that made her feel secure when he was about? What was the difference between the young chemist and Paul that she felt perfect trust in the one whom she had known only a short time and distrust and uncertainty in the other to whom she was about to be married?

She hung her head and went into the drawing-room, leaving Paul standing there. He looked after her, and a slight smile crossed his face as he thought of what a fool she was to think that he cared for her. His self-assurance led him to believe that the reason that Eva was not consenting to his proposal was indeed because of her father's condition, for he little dreamed, nor would his egotism permit him to believe, that anything else could be the case.

His mouth hardened in a subtle smile as he sauntered after Eva to bid her farewell. He remembered that De Luxe Dora was waiting outside for him in her speedster.

He had made this paramour of his take him to the very door of his fiancee's home, and there wait until he had paid his respects to the moneyed lady who would make happiness possible by supplying him with the funds to pursue his pleasures and insure his father's hold on the International Patents, Incorporated.

Paul looked at his watch, then, after a few words of condolence which would hardly sound sincere from any one less gifted, made a hurried departure toward the corner where the speedster was waiting.

"Who was the funny gink that hurried by a little while ago?" queried Dora, in the vernacular of her calling. "He gave me the double O as though he had something on me."

"That's a fellow we've got to look out for, kid," answered Paul, in the same terms by which he was addressed, for, if nothing else, Paul could be as much at home in the underworld as in a mansion on the Drive. "Brent claimed that he was a chemist before he went 'bugs,'" continued Paul, "but I have my doubts; in fact, I'm very leery of him because I think he's a fly cop."

He took his place beside Dora, who started the car and headed down-town.

After Paul's departure Eva hurried to her father's room and

tried to comfort him. He was seated in a chair, staring blankly ahead of him. He was quieter now, but his body twitched nervously from time to time.

The tears started to come to Eva's eyes as she saw her father's plight, and she knelt down beside him and took his hand in hers. She stroked it with her own hand and bent over and kissed it. As she knelt, crying softly, she sobbed half-aloud:

"Why can't I confide in you, father? Why can't you advise me? I don't love Paul Balcom and could never marry him. I know I love Quentin Locke—I do—I do—"

As she sobbed she bent over his hand and pressed it to her lips.

Peter Brent sat staring into space, staring like a graven image.

CHAPTER VII

After her brief encounter with Balcom in the hallway Zita stealthily mounted to Flint's room.

Flint's condition was unchanged. He lay sprawled out in a huge arm-chair, his head swaying from side to side, as he muttered and mumbled incoherently, while his leering smile caused even Zita to shudder.

She was, however, alive to the importance of her mission. Steeling herself, she raised Flint from the chair and steadied him with one hand while she tried to smooth out the wrinkles of his clothing so that his mad condition would not be too apparent when they went outdoors. It was a hard task, but Zita soon accomplished it and, half supporting, she led him through a door on the farther side of the room. They crept down a back stairway and so away from the house.

At times Flint stumbled and almost fell, and once that insane laugh startled a passer-by, who started after them, then changed his mind and proceeded on his way. It was then that Zita's heart almost stopped beating. She realized that the situation would be unexplainable to a stranger and she urged the insane Flint on faster.

Renewed hope came to her with each step. She had almost

relaxed her precautions when, suddenly, from a clump of bushes, several men leaped out. They seized Flint, who merely started babbling afresh. Zita, ignorant of what was really happening, struck out right and left in the hopeless encounter, until one of the men with a grin seized her wrist in his powerful grasp and twisted it until she screamed with pain. Then she realized for the first time that she had fallen into the hands of the emissaries of the Automaton. Had Balcom planned it, or had that mechanical monster taken advantage of what Balcom had ordered?

In the mean time, the other thugs, with Flint between them, made off hurriedly. With a last push that almost threw Zita to the ground, the last of them dashed into the shrubbery, and for several moments Zita dazedly stood there as he crashed through the underbrush, making good the escape and capture. Then she turned and ran back to Brent Rock.

Locke, in the mean time, had arrived at the laboratory of his old friend Hadwell, the chemist, where he was warmly welcomed.

It was the usual dusty workshop of one devoted to one idea—science—with no touches of comfort. Hadwell fairly lived amid retorts, Bunsen burners, and reagents.

He was a man of profound research, rather than the commercial chemist, and it was from him that Locke, in earlier days, had learned many lessons so well that now his career was watched with interest by many distinguished men of science.

Hadwell was delighted at the chance to examine the strange scrapings of wax which Locke had dug out of the sockets of the candlestick, the more so as they must contain some mysterious poison. First he studied them under a powerful lens, then by chemical reactions, until he made visible some

Arthur B. Reeve and John W. Grey

peculiar crystals. Locke himself was amazed as his friend worked.

"You don't know it all—yet—my boy," smiled the aged professor. "There's still something the old teacher can add to your education, and I'm glad, Quentin, very glad, for it will draw you closer to me again. I need you to carry on my work when I must lay it down. I'm not positive," he continued, "but I believe these crystals to be those of *Dhatura stramonium*, and, as you say speed's the thing, we'll begin by noting the effect of the stuff as a gas on that guinea-pig over there."

"Have you masks?" asked Locke, with true scientific caution.

"Yes—on the shelf. You're keen, Quentin. These fumes can penetrate the tiniest aperture and, if my guess is right, without a mask, you would quickly laugh yourself to death."

"Don't, Professor, don't joke, for there is no joy in that mad laughter. It is horrible, maddening, even to the hearer. Let us get to work. The father of the girl I love may even now be sinking to his death. We must determine the nature of this deadly stuff, and then find an antidote."

The chemist brought out the cage in which the guinea-pig was placidly munching a lettuce leaf, and placed it in a convenient spot on the table. Then, after Locke, as well as the professor, had carefully adjusted the masks, the latter lighted a Bunsen burner and applied the flame to the deadly crystals. A pungent fume was given off and collected in a rubber bag, or cone, from which a long tube protruded.

This tube the chemist introduced into the cage. For a moment there was no perceptible change in the animal's actions. Then it stopped eating, sniffed at the strange odor, and commenced to twitch violently. This twitching continued for several minutes, when the creature started to revolve in circles, like a Japanese dancing-mouse. Finally it became subject to spasms, and, although the professor withdrew the tube, these symptoms continued.

"I was right!" he cried. "It is an especially poisonous variety of that almost unknown Oriental drug, *Dhatura stramonium*. I think I can find an antidote to it, also. To work, my boy, to work!"

One experiment after another resulted in failure, however, and it was while they were so engaged that the telephone bell rang and a feminine voice inquired for Locke.

It was an excited Eva who called. "Quentin," she burst forth, breathlessly, "what do you think has happened? The strangest thing! Flint has escaped. Tell me what to do. Can't you come to me at once? I need you."

Locke needed no further urging. Important though the work of finding the antidote was, Eva's call was more imperative to him. He reassured her as best he could over the wire, for he had no idea what had really happened. Zita, as might have been expected, on her return to Brent Rock had been far too clever to disclose the exact truth that Flint had been abducted, and that while in her own charge.

When she arrived at Brent Rock she had mounted by the same stairway by which she and Flint had departed. Entering Flint's room, she had raised the alarm and had acted her part so well that Eva thought that she had discovered Flint's absence at the precise moment at which Zita had cried out and she had come running in answer to her call.

Locke gave Hadwell a brief outline of what had just

occurred at Brent Rock.

"Professor," he pleaded, "for Heaven's sake don't fail me. Try as you never tried before to find the antidote for this strange combination of poisons. Telephone me when you have it."

Locke seized his hat, and Hadwell redoubled his efforts to fathom the toxic secret.

At Brent Rock, in the mean time, everything was in confusion, Eva was almost distracted, and, to add to her discomfort, Paul took occasion to call.

In the past few days her distrust of him, for she could call it by no other name, had grown, and the furtive glances which he exchanged with Zita, little trouble-maker, were not reassuring. But when Eva's maid, motioning her aside, told her that she had been a witness to the departure of Zita and Flint, Eva's suspicions from a vague misgiving became a stern reality. She longed for Locke's return and protection from the very man to whom she was engaged.

As Locke left the chemist's he noticed a light runabout across the street, half hidden in the shadows. But he failed to notice the evil face of De Luxe Dora peering at him from beneath the rim of a well-pulled-down hat.

"Huh!" she muttered. "We'll get his number and here's where I go after it."

Locke hailed a passing taxicab, gave a hurried direction to the chauffeur, and jumped in. The taxi snorted, cut out open, and jumped forward as the driver clumsily shifted the worn gears. But out of the shadows there glided a low-hung runabout with a purling motor that without effort kept Locke's taxi just in sight without seeming to be following.

At the time that the emissaries abducted Flint he had been roughly handled and some of his clothing had been torn. But as he had been incapable of the slightest degree of real self-defense, the thugs had soon desisted beating him up, with the result that he had escaped bodily injury except for a few slight scratches.

The emissaries of the Automaton led him by devious winding paths down to the shore, and, half walking, half running, pressing close to the high cliffs, they urged him forward.

Soon they came to a cleft in the rock, and, with one hand using a well-hooded electric torch to light the way, they dragged the poor unfortunate into the cave entrance to the den.

This cave was a marvel of nature, hewn out of the solid rock by countless tides, its dome lost in the darkness. It gave an impression of immensity, while in many directions passage-ways gave off from what might be called a main chamber.

Flint was roughly thrown on a rock, where, head in hands, he swayed backward and forward, now moaning, now chuckling, now laughing outright. The echo of that laugh resounded hollowly in the dismal place and must have notified the supreme master of this underground world that his domain had been invaded.

A metallic clanging in the distance, as of struck anvils, a crunching, as the smaller rocks broke in twain under the enormous weight of the iron monster, then far, far down the passageway two points of fire—the eyes of the thing—and with arms swinging like flails, from out the passageway there stalked—the Automaton.

Even the emissaries, slaves to this monster through fear, and seeing it often, fell back in awe and consternation, so terrible was its menace.

It strode over to Flint and, pushing him backward, glared at him with burning eyes that seemed to search his soul. The monster then turned to one of the emissaries and, with a sweeping gesture, gave a command.

The emissary understood and immediately ran up one of the passageways, returning in a few moments with a bottle which contained a purplish mixture. At another sign from the Automaton the emissary took a drinking-glass and poured out a portion of the purple fluid. Then he forced the draught between Flint's clenched teeth.

A violent trembling shook Flint from head to foot, a shudder of so exhausting a nature that after the spasm Flint, weakened, reclined against the cold wall of the cave, his body in a clammy perspiration. But gradually there came a change in his dazed, mad eyes. The iris contracted and became more normal. Even the leaden hue of his face slowly passed away. The face muscles relaxed and gradually the light of reason appeared in his eyes.

In a questioning manner Flint gazed about him. He saw the cave with its scintillating points of fire, as the man with the torch gesticulated. He saw the emissaries, and the realization that his position was perilous came to him. But it was only when he saw the towering form of the Automaton that his blood froze with horror and he made a frantic effort to escape the very thing which he had feared existed in Madagascar and had attempted to betray to Brent on the fatal night.

It was useless. He was soon borne down by the thugs, who stationed two of their number to guard him. Seeing the utter hopelessness of any attempt to escape, Flint sat quietly, while his crafty mind schemed for some other plan. Suddenly he saw the bottle, the contents of which had restored his reason. Reaching out slyly, he turned it around until he could read the label, and then, even in his predicament, he exulted over his discovery. It was the antidote. Like a flash came to him a shrewd scheme to use the knowledge.

An emissary who seemed to be a leader came over to him.

"Flint," he snarled, "you get one chance—see? Beat it back to Brent Rock and see that you get that Brent girl to come to the place where we will turn you loose. Understand? If you fail it means death. Think it over."

Flint could only agree.

They bandaged his eyes and quickly led him back over the road by which they had come.

CHAPTER VIII

Brent Rock was brilliantly lighted against Locke's coming. At the foot of the great stairway a group of excited servants had gathered, as if for mutual protection.

"Not another day will I stay in this house," quavered the cook. "What with crazy laughing and the other carryings-on, I'm fair distracted."

"Take shame to yerself, Mary Dolan, for yer gab of quittin', with the master and Miss Eva in sore trouble," answered the second girl. "But as you say," she continued, shaking her head, "it's a gloomy old place, and if it wasn't for Miss Eva I'd not be long in going myself."

"'Ave you no loyalty?" asked the butler, turning on them both.

"Hould yer jaw, Johnny Bull," threatened the cook. "Indade no foreigner can tell Mary Dolan her duty."

So they wrangled back and forth, and the underlying cause of all the discord was the old one—fear.

Nor was Eva exempt from its baneful influence. She was here, there, everywhere, allaying one servant's apprehension, commanding another to perform some task in order to occupy that servant's mind—but, for herself, she knew that the strain would not lessen until Locke arrived. She ran upstairs and to a window from which she could obtain a better view of the drive along which he must come.

In a very short time, which, nevertheless, seemed an age to her, Eva was rewarded, and she fairly flew down the stairs, out of the house, and far down the drive. Locke's taxi stopped, he leaped out, and, regardless of the chauffeur, took Eva's hand.

"Tell me quickly what has happened?" he inquired.

From a distance Dora was a witness, exulting.

"Paul stands a swell chance with her," she sneered.

"Oh, I'm so glad you're here," confided Eva, letting down just a bit of her restraint as, like a frightened child, she told of what she had learned about the disappearance of Flint.

Locke dismissed the driver, and together they walked slowly toward the house.

Not only Eva, but the entire household was relieved by Locke's presence. The cook rushed forward and, with a "God bless you, sir!" would have embraced him had he not stepped aside. Even the dignified old family butler tried to take his hand, an unheard-of liberty on his part. For, unknowingly, all had come suddenly to rely upon this quiet, unassuming young man.

Locke immediately asked to be shown to Flint's room in the hope that Flint might have left some clue behind. But, although they searched high and low, no success met their efforts.

It was then that they faced their darkest moment. Feeling, as they did, that they were encircled by hidden enemies, the very air they breathed became a menace. Every attempt to find the thread that might unravel the dark mystery proved futile. It was not to be wondered at that they despaired. Even the weird laughter of Eva's stricken father, echoing hollowly through the house, seemed to be mocking their efforts.

The Automaton's emissaries were anxious to do their job and return to the cave, for, like rats, they preferred the security best found underground. They did not lead Flint very far.

At the edge of the Brent estate there was an Italian marble fountain decorated with bronze dolphins and water-nymphs disporting themselves. It was at this fountain that the men halted Flint and, with a final warning, left him.

For a few moments, such was his fear, Flint did not remove the bandage from his eyes, but moved groping around until his hand came in contact with the edge of the fountain. For a moment he stood quietly, listening for sounds of the emissaries. Then, as he heard nothing, he tore the bandage from his eyes, gazed wonderingly around him until his mind grasped his exact location, then, with a bound, started to run toward Brent Rock.

Had he noticed the bestial face of an emissary peering from the shrubbery he would have been even more frightened. Retribution, he would have known, would be swift and sure had he disregarded their commands and moved in another direction.

As Flint left the fountain Balcom, suave and well groomed as usual, was just giving his hat and stick to the butler when Locke and Eva, returning from Flint's room, encountered him in the hallway.

"Oh, Mr. Balcom," exclaimed Eva, "Mr. Locke and I are at a loss to account for Mr. Flint's disappearance! I told the gardeners, and they have hunted for him all over the estate and beyond, but he has disappeared as completely as though the ground had swallowed him."

Balcom expressed his utmost astonishment and at once insisted on going to Flint's room to solve the mystery himself.

Eva and Locke went directly into the library, where Locke for the first time had an opportunity to tell Eva the result of his visit to the chemist. The fact that they had discovered the nature of the toxin was in itself encouraging, and Eva felt that, even now, she could see the glimmer of a silver lining to the clouds.

"If we can only locate Mr. Flint, Quentin," she murmured, "I feel that much would be explained."

Hardly had the words passed her lips when, breathless and disheveled, Flint staggered up the stairs from under the porte-cochere and into the hallway. Balcom, just descending from his brief inspection of Flint's room, hailed him.

"What has happened?" he demanded. "Don't go into the library."

"I've just escaped from the Automaton," shouted Flint, "and I've found the antidote!"

Before Balcom could stop him he rushed into the library, Balcom following in a towering rage. Eva gave a startled little cry at the wild intrusion and Locke moved closer to her.

"Is the antidote that will restore your father's reason worth ten thousand dollars to you?" demanded Flint; then, before Eva could reply, added: "Speak quick! I've got to get out of the country to-night."

"Ten thousand!" gasped Eva. "Ten times ten thousand! Tell me what it is."

"Show me the money first," haggled Flint, "and remember I must have the hard cash."

"Just a moment, Eva," interrupted Locke. "Consider this thing well. We can deal with this fellow as a final resort."

Eva looked from Locke to Balcom, her mind in a turmoil, as the telephone-bell rang and Locke hurried to answer it.

In the room now there was a conflict of emotions and desires that fairly electrified the place. Eva ardently craved her father's recovery at all costs. Flint's avaricious mind wavered between a scheme nearing success and the possibility of failure and the fear of the Automaton. Balcom strained to hear the purport of the message that Locke was receiving.

At the sound of the chemist's voice Locke was tense with suppressed excitement.

"I've found the antidote," hastened to report the professor.

With a cordial word of thanks Locke turned from the telephone and faced the group in the room. As he made the announcement, Eva almost embraced him in the flood of relief at the thought of her father restored.

"Eva," growled Balcom, "you forget yourself. As Paul's father, I cannot countenance such actions."

"Mr. Balcom," interrupted Locke, "I am sure you will be kind in your criticism of Miss Brent. She has merely overrated my service to her."

"Paul shall hear of this," stormed Balcom.

"If your son cares to take the matter up with me," returned Locke, now on his dignity, "I am always to be found— here."

"Never mind," interposed Flint, who feared to see his chance slipping, "I've got to get out of the country. Mr. Locke, your antidote is probably valueless; mine is the certain one. Look at me, Miss Brent. Am I not cured?"

"You miserable sneak," scowled Locke, stepping over to him, "we don't need your assistance now."

"I'm dealing with Miss Brent," insisted Flint, insolently.

Eva, a bit nervous over Balcom's overbearing manner, interposed. "Mr. Locke," she said, with just a touch of dignity for effect on Balcom, "this is a matter of life and death, and I am not in favor of permitting a proven antidote to be taken out of the country by this—this man. I have every confidence in you, but suppose—just suppose—that your chemist friend is mistaken."

Flint immediately saw his advantage and pressed it home. "Are you going to let ten thousand dollars stand in the way of your father's recovery?" he insinuated. "Here," he added, taking pencil and paper from his pocket and writing hurriedly.

"Baker's dock," Eva read, as he handed her the paper, "until five o'clock."

Arthur B. Reeve and John W. Grey

Flint bowed decently enough to her, glanced upward, and, as he thought of Eva's father lying stricken with the Madagascar madness in the room above, an evil leer came over his fox-like face. As he left he completely ignored both Locke and Balcom, unless it was that the look in his eyes meant a sort of sinister triumph.

Locke followed him out of the library, and for a few moments Eva and Balcom were alone.

Balcom had been quick to realize that it would not further his plans if he continued to antagonize this high-spirited girl. He took another course. The kind and fatherly manner which he could assume so readily was now apparent.

"Eva, my dear child," he ingratiated, "I am really sorry for the hasty way in which I spoke, but, aside from our duty to International Patents, your marriage to my son has been my greatest hope and ambition."

"I can't see why you should wish a daughter-in-law of whose actions you disapprove," retorted Eva, pointedly.

It was a facer for Balcom and he quickly guided the conversation into less dangerous channels.

Eva's candid nature could not comprehend treachery of any kind in others, and yet, although she was unable to put a name to it, she had a vague feeling of insecurity in dealing with her father's partner. This feeling had been heightened by Balcom's actions. In speaking of the proposed marriage to Paul he had come quite close to her. She shuddered, for, out of the corner of her eye, only a few moments before, she remembered him in the same position when Flint had handed her the address, and she knew that Balcom had surreptitiously read it. Why had he taken that underhand method when, if he had only asked frankly to see the paper, she would have handed it to him without hesitation or suspicion.

Eva started to leave the library, but Balcom stopped her with a gesture. "My dear," he said, "your father is stricken with a deadly malady. His affairs are in your hands to protect his interests. I must urge that you marry Paul at the earliest possible moment."

Eva scarcely knew what to say. "I can't," she blurted out, then tried to cover her confusion and made it worse, "only—as a last resort—to save my father—Oh—good-by!" And she almost ran from the room.

CHAPTER IX

Meanwhile, as Flint left Brent Rock, his fear of the Automaton returned to him with redoubled force. He had been false to his mission. Nor had he even succeeded in his treachery. A few minutes he had been certain that Eva would come to Baker's dock at the time set, but now doubts began to assail him. With her obvious faith in Locke, she might decide on the chemist's antidote, and there was always a possibility that it might restore Brent, in which case Flint realized that his life would be forfeit to the Automaton.

Nor were his fears unfounded. He had barely passed the fountain where, half an hour before, he had been set free, when an emissary came out from behind a neighboring tree and took up his trail.

De Luxe Dora also had waited only long enough to see Eva and Locke enter Brent Rock, when she turned her runabout around and drove rapidly back to Professor Hadwell's. She arrived there just in time to meet an automobile coming from the opposite direction and containing three emissaries of the Automaton.

In answer to an inquiry, Dora pointed out the chemist's house to them. They piled out, and their leader knocked at the door, while Dora drove off.

The chemist answered, and the leader produced a vial, glibly lying as he handed it over.

"The Williams Drug Company sent me to have this stuff analyzed," said the leader. "I'll wait."

As the professor admitted him he did not see the other two men pressed close to the wall on either side of the door. The moment the professor's back was turned they slinked after their leader into the house. In a dark corner of the hallway they crouched as their leader went into the laboratory with the chemist.

The professor sniffed at the vial, which contained nothing but pure water, and in surprise turned to the emissary for an explanation. But it was too late. The emissary dealt him a blow with a blunt instrument that stunned him and, as he reeled back and grasped at a table, the other thugs rushed from the hall and rained blow after blow on his venerable head and beat him to the floor. A convulsive shudder—a long-drawn-out sigh—and he lay still.

With barely a glance at him the emissaries set to work to smash all the paraphernalia of the place, sparing nothing in order to make sure that the antidote would be destroyed. Glass tubes, retorts, bottles, even furniture were smashed to bits in their orgy of ruin—and there, in the midst of the debris, his life's work finished, lay the old chemist, dead.

Tiring of their own efforts, the murderers at last desisted. One of them went to the street door and peered out, but in a moment was back with the others.

"Quick—that fellow Locke is coming."

He was right. Locke had immediately quit Brent Rock and had come directly to the chemist's in the hope of forestalling any further attempt by Flint to inveigle Eva into dealing with him.

The door had been left ajar and, although he thought it strange, Locke was without suspicion and entered the hallway. He called to his old friend, but the dead lips could not answer and the emissaries would not.

Greatly alarmed now, Locke strode to the laboratory. For a moment he stood as though petrified as the horrid scene burst upon his vision. He ran to the chemist and knelt beside his battered body.

With a rush the emissaries darted from their hiding-place and were upon him.

Although taken unawares, Locke was, in a measure, ready for them. One he grabbed in a clever jiu-jitsu hold and sent him hurtling through the air to crash in a heap in a far corner of the room. Leaping to his feet, he beat another to the floor. The third villain was of tougher fiber. Up and down the laboratory they battled, stumbling over broken furniture, now falling to the floor, where they rolled over and over, first one, then the other gaining the mastery, while the broken glass with which the floor was littered cut their clothing to ribbons and bit into their flesh.

Locke was slowly gaining the upper hand when the thug whom he had thrown over his head recovered. The brute took the situation in at a glance, saw his pal in trouble, and, sneaking treacherously behind Locke, dealt him a terrific blow with the butt of a revolver. Locke dropped to the floor as if pole-axed and lay still.

One of the thugs kicked him as he lay defenseless, and then, spying a row of coat-hooks in an inner hallway, with fiendish ingenuity directed the others who had joined him.

They strung Locke up by his thumbs so that he hung, half suspended, with his toes just off the floor.

As one of them searched him Locke was still unconscious. They found nothing but a few bank-notes and the automatic revolver that Locke always carried.

Slowly Locke regained his senses. The agony of his strained thumbs was almost unbearable. But he was not the man to give up.

By this time two of the emissaries had gone, leaving one, who seated himself quite close to Locke, where he was examining the revolver. With the stoicism of an Indian, Locke manfully tried to evolve a plan by which he might escape. Like a flash it came to him, but it was a plan so fraught with the possibility of failure that he would not have decided on it except for the agony of the strain on his thumbs.

Directly opposite him and at a distance of four or five feet was a door leading to a back alley. This door the emissary now guarding him had locked as a precaution against surprise and had carefully placed the key in his vest pocket.

Locke weighed each detail of his plan and then, bracing his feet firmly against the wall, he suddenly shot his lower limbs forward and, like the closing of a pair of giant shears, he wrapped his legs about the neck of the emissary and immediately exerted enormous pressure with his knees.

The emissary, taken totally by surprise, struggled to break the hold, and Locke's thumbs were almost wrenched from their sockets. But he held on grimly. Soon the thug's struggles subsided, Locke released him, and he slipped to the floor.

Arthur B. Reeve and John W. Grey

Locke was wearing a low-cut shoe. Strange that a man's life may hinge on such a slight detail, but this fact enabled him to work off his right shoe and his sock. He extended his bare foot, and with his toes searched the pocket of the emissary for the key to the door. Finally he found it.

Locke held the key as firmly as he might between his toes and, projecting his body by a muscular effort far away from the wall, he managed to insert the key in the lock. He turned it. The door was unlocked now. A swift downward movement of his foot against the knob and the door swung open.

He braced himself against its edge and, with his back firmly pressed against the wall, relieved the strain on his thumbs. He rested a moment and then, as it were, walked up the edge of the door until his feet reached the top. Swinging one leg over the door, by patient effort he was enabled to release one swollen thumb, then the other. An instant later he dropped down and leaned exhaustedly against the wall.

While Locke was held in the room things had happened which would have set him nearly crazy with anxiety. Eva, having heard nothing from him, had become alarmed and had telephoned to the chemist. This was at quarter to five, and she had supposed that it was the chemist who answered her. In reality it had been an emissary, and he had told her that the final experiment to find an antidote for her father's malady had been really a failure and that Locke had left some time before.

After all that she had endured, this was almost the final blow to Eva. She thought of Flint and Baker's dock and five o'clock. There was no time to lose if she were to save her father. So she pulled herself together, seized her hat and cloak, and started for the door.

Here Zita stopped her and offered to accompany her, but she declined. She hastily asked the direction of Baker's dock from the butler, and then ran out of the house and sprang to the steering-wheel of her waiting car. With a whir of the starter she was away.

Flint had arrived at the dock long before and was now slinking in and out among the crates and boxes as he sought diligently for a safe hiding-place. But his nerves, none too strong at the best, were now running riot, and nowhere could he feel a sense of security so that he could remain quiet.

It was while he was sneaking from one pile of bales to another that an emissary hailed him.

"Are you Flint?" he demanded.

"Y-e-s," came quaveringly from Flint.

"Well, there's a lady in the office asking for you."

Such was the fascination of any of the emissaries of the Automaton over Flint by this time that he followed the man without question, particularly as he felt that he would be spared, since the lady in the office could be none other than Eva.

Together they walked toward the entrance and, with an order to wait, the emissary halted Flint close to a pile of crates and left him. Flint dared not move. A premonition of impending disaster must have come over him, for his knees shook and a clammy sweat broke out on his forehead.

Without sound a gigantic iron hand and arm protruded from behind a crate and, for a moment, hung suspended over Flint's head. Then, with a swift encircling movement,

Arthur B. Reeve and John W. Grey

that hooklike arm wrapped itself around Flint's neck and drew him into the shadow. The mighty form drew the victim close—and it was over.

The Automaton picked up the body as though it had been a mere feather-weight and stalked out to the waiting emissaries. A trap-door was opened and Flint's body was dashed into the river. Thus it was that all his scheming came to an end and his secret from Madagascar, which he had told Brent, but which now lay locked in that mad-man's mind, was stilled with Flint's dead lips.

At the chemist's shop Locke was by this time recovering from the terrible ordeal through which he had passed. He bathed his swollen thumbs, and by rubbing them was able somewhat to restore the circulation. Then he stepped to the telephone and gave the Brent Rock number.

It was Zita who answered him.

"Eva has gone alone to Baker's dock," she answered to his inquiry, in half-triumphant jealousy.

Locke did not wait to hear more. There was not a moment to be lost. He rushed out, disheveled as he was, into the street, slamming the door after him. It seemed hours before he could find a taxicab.

"Baker's dock!" he yelled. "And twenty dollars if you make it in ten minutes."

He did not know that the emissaries had robbed him of everything, nor would it have made any difference, for he could easily have fixed it with the driver through his police and Secret Service connections.

In the mean time Eva's car had met with misfortune, and

she had been compelled to stop. She jumped out and busied herself with a missing cylinder.

Locke's taxi was running smoothly and arrived at the dock well within the time he had ordered. Locke jumped out and started to pay. It was then that he discovered that he was without money. The driver became angry and hard to pacify with the story of the robbery, but Locke finally convinced him that all was right with the Department of Justice.

Locke walked through the gates to the dock and for a moment stood nonplussed. This dock had none of the turmoil and bustle naturally associated with docks when a steamer is about to leave.

He cautiously proceeded between the piles of merchandise toward the end of the wharf. Of one thing he was now certain and a prayer of relief came to his lips. He was there before Eva and able to guard her from any danger that might arise.

His eyes were keen, but he failed to notice the emissaries who, from behind crates and bales, were watching his every move. Nor did he see that fiend of iron, the Automaton, which, standing rigid, glared at him from behind an enormous packing-case.

He continued down the wharf as, slinking like coyotes, those sinister forms glided from hiding-place to hiding-place and were never far from his heels. He reached the end of the wharf and gazed up and down the dark river. Here and there he could distinguish the colored lights that marked a tugboat or some other small craft, but of a large steamer there was no sign. It is rarely that a boat warps into a dock just a few moments before leaving for foreign parts, and it flashed upon Locke's mind that Flint had deceived them about his leaving for Madagascar that night.

Arthur B. Reeve and John W. Grey

He was still wondering what it could all mean when the emissaries leaped upon him. Although weakened by his previous battle, Locke proved no easy customer for them. Time after time he struggled free from them and with arms working like piston-rods for a while he kept them at a distance. But, like a pack of wolves, they were not to be denied, and they finally succeeded in holding him firmly.

One of them brought leg-irons which he snapped around Locke's ankles. Once again Locke managed to get one of his arms free and, before they could prevent him, two emissaries lay prostrate on the wharf. But that effort marked his last, for the Automaton, stalking up behind him, pinioned his arms as though he was a baby.

An emissary now placed a pair of handcuffs on his wrists and, to bind him more securely, fastened a chain that extended from the handcuffs to the leg-irons.

Two of the thugs now carried him to the edge of the wharf, while a third attached a heavy weight to Locke's feet. Locke realized his helplessness, realized that his death was imminent. But he determined to rid the world of at least one murderer. By a mighty effort he shook off his captors and, as one rushed forward, he grabbed him in his manacled hands and leaped with him into the river as they grappled.

At the shore end of the wharf an emissary was leading Eva, as she thought, to Flint.

Locke and the thug sank immediately to the bottom of the river and, under water, there ensued a terrific battle. Locke, semi-helpless because of his shakles, had the greatest difficulty in preventing the thug from breaking loose. But he was determined that the fellow at least would pay for his crimes with his life.

The thug's struggles gradually became more feeble. Air bubbles rose from his bestial lips and he became limp in Locke's grasp. Locke released him and, feet first, he floated upward, dead.

Locke's lungs were almost bursting now as he struggled at his chains; his senses reeled; he thought of Eva, and redoubled his efforts. If he could only get rid of that great weight that was holding him down. A singing came in his ears.

CHAPTER X

As Eva hurried down the dock, looking for the renegade, Flint she found herself cornered between the emissary and the terrible Automaton himself. With a scream of terror she ran until she came to a door that divided the dock into fireproof sections. Through it she darted, the Automaton following relentlessly.

Meanwhile Locke, his lungs almost bursting and the blood surging to his head, had managed to free himself from his shackles and had floated to the surface of the water. As he came up he swam to the piles of the dock just as several boatmen saw him and hurried to his aid.

They heard the screams of Eva, and all started running up the dock, but not in time to capture the Automaton, who, warned by the emissaries, crashed through the side of the dock house nearest the shore and escaped.

A moment later Locke, searching through the piles of boxes, bales, and crates, found Eva, just recovering from her fright, and in the joy of having saved her by his timely return forgot, for the moment, to pursue the terrible villain, who managed to reach a waiting closed car and was whisked away.

Thus it was that after their return to Brent Rock, on the

following day Eva was ministering to her father, still hopelessly insane through the failure to discover the antidote to the madness.

While Eva was engaged in her ministrations up-stairs Locke was finishing some experiment in his laboratory. Down-stairs, Balcom had just arrived in the hall, where he was met by Zita with a report of what had happened the day before.

"Tell it to me in the strong-room while I place this package there," Balcom whispered, indicating the package which he had brought.

Together Balcom and Zita descended to the cellar and made their way to the Graveyard of Genius as Zita poured forth her story, unmindful of the fact that the butler had seen them go down and was watching very skeptically. In the Graveyard Balcom unwrapped a small model of a motor and placed it on the shelf.

Eva, having left her father, came upon Locke in the hall, and there they stood talking for a moment, when the butler approached apologetically.

"Begging your pardon, Miss Brent," he reported, "but I just saw Mr. Balcom go down to the strong-room with Miss Zita, and I thought you might like to know."

"Thank you," nodded Eva, dismissing the butler and trying to show no concern in the matter.

But Locke shot a quick glance at her as the servant left, and it was evident that both felt the same suspicion, for Locke immediately excused himself and hurried down-stairs.

In the Graveyard Balcom and Zita were talking in subdued tones as Zita whispered.

"I suppose you know," she nodded, "that before Mr. Brent went mad he wrote a confession with a list of these inventions which International Patents has suppressed?"

Balcom could scarcely conceal his rage. "Yes, I know it," he replied, savagely. "That confession would cause a great deal of trouble."

Low as they were talking, they would have been even more careful had they known that Locke was listening outside and that, even as they turned to leave the strong-room, he had sidled out of the way and was rejoining Eva in the library.

Locke had scarcely told Eva what he had heard when she moved over to the safe and would have tried to open it had he not stopped her. For he had heard the other two coming from the cellar, and even as it was they were at the hall door.

"My dear," remarked Balcom as he entered and went to Eva, "since your father is not likely to recover, I must ask you to transfer all the company papers from his private safe to the office of the company."

Eva did not respond to the fatherly manner assumed by Balcom. Instead she almost point-blank refused to do as he had requested.

Just then Locke, whom Balcom had almost ignored up to the present, heard the noise of some one coming through the conservatory. It was Paul Balcom, his coat on his arm, his sleeves rolled up, and a tennis-racquet in his hand, as he had come just from the courts.

Paul glanced surlily at Locke, who bowed pleasantly to him, as well he might, considering their relative positions in Eva's real affections. Catching sight of his father with Eva, Paul paused a moment.

It was just at that instant that Balcom had been saying to her: "Why don't you marry Paul, as you promised your father and me? That would settle all the difficulties."

Paul had suspected the nature of the conversation, though he approached as if ignorant of it. Apparently catching the drift, he deftly urged her, but Eva tactfully changed the subject, greatly to Paul's chagrin and his father's ill-suppressed anger.

The suspense of the situation was relieved for Eva by the nearer approach of Locke, who must have had some inkling of what was going on. Paul and his father exchanged glances as the young chemist and detective joined Eva, and it was evident that no love toward him was wasted by either.

"Excuse me," she apologized, walking away with Locke, "but there is something very important that I must attend to for my father's interests."

Locke and Eva walked to the safe, while Balcom and Paul watched like hawks.

A moment later Eva was kneeling before the safe, after giving Locke a paper which contained the combination numbers to open the bolts. Locke glanced at it, then held it where Eva could read:

Combination of Safe
Turn once left to 40
Three right to 18
Once left to 40

As Locke held the paper and Eva's slender hand spun the combination lock, Balcom and Paul moved silently forward. Although Locke was holding the paper with the combinations for Eva, he heard them come up behind him and knew that they were watching. With a quiet smile to himself he moved the paper over so that they could see it, nor were they slow to take advantage of the chance. Locke's mind was working fast, and he had a purpose in what seemed to be carelessness or even foolishness.

A moment later Eva opened the safe and from it she took a typewritten document of many pages.

It read:

BOARD OF DIRECTORS,

International Patents, Inc.,
New York.

GENTLEMEN,—In view of the government's anti-trust investigation, I have prepared this list of inventions we have suppressed. I think we should discuss at our annual meeting the advisability of surrendering our rights to these inventions, no matter what may happen to the corporations we have been protecting.

Very truly yours,

PETER BRENT.

Following this letter was a bulky paper, or rather set of papers, which detailed the inventions and their history, exposing some of the nefarious operations of the corporation.

Balcom, as he read the top letter, showed great agitation. As Locke took the package from Eva, Balcom interrupted:

"That's very dangerous," he said. "If it gets out, the corporations are ruined."

Locke scarcely replied. Instead, he very ostentatiously replaced the document in the safe, refusing to intrust it either to Balcom or to Paul, who withdrew sullenly, leaving Eva alone with Locke in the library as Locke whirled the combination of the closed safe door.

It was perhaps half an hour later in the secret den of the Automaton in the rock-hewn foundation of Brent Rock that the emissaries were watching the arched and dark passage. Suddenly there was the warning clank, and the huge steel monster strode in.

For some time he stood before the table, giving his instructions by means of mysterious, cryptic motions.

Meantime, above in Brent Rock, Locke had been busy, for he had conceived an entirely new plan to capture the Automaton. It was nothing short of an electric trap, and deadly in its simplicity.

From the wall switch Locke had led wires carrying the house current. Already, also, he had let Eva in on his secret plan, and she was all eagerness as he planted his trap.

Before the safe, now, Locke paused, and there for a moment twisted the combination so that he could get his correct position. That done, he noted the place where he had been standing, and removed a mat from the floor in front of the safe. At that place he set in on the floor a fairly large iron plate. To this iron plate he attached a wire, then replaced the rug, but in such a way that a part of the plate was exposed, though it would never be noticed.

"If the Automaton attempts to open the safe," he remarked to Eva, as he worked, "he will complete the electric circuit and it will hold him until we capture him."

"How clever!" Eva exclaimed, involuntarily.

"Now for making my signaling connection to the laboratory," continued Locke. "Then I must get some of my men up here from the department."

However, while Locke and Eva were busy arranging this electric trap, they did not notice that they were being watched by Zita, who had stolen into the conservatory and was eying them eagerly from the protection of the fronds of a palm. Zita, moreover, was greatly excited, as she gathered with her quick perception just what it was that they were doing. Nor did she wait to see the work finished, but stole out of the door and away hurriedly.

Locke had finished his preparations, and as he and Eva were discussing the possibilities of what he had devised, he remarked, in answer to her eager inquiry about his suspicions, "I am sure we shall prove that there is a man inside the terrible machine that attacks us."

"Then you don't think it is really an automaton?" asked Eva, with great respect for Locke's opinion, though it was sufficiently in evidence that she was not at all convinced that the monster was not really of steel and controlled by something that resembled a human brain.

Locke was non-committal. "This trap will tell us," was all that he would say.

Zita, hurrying out from the conservatory, and wishing to waste not an instant in notifying Balcom, sought a near-by telephone pay-station, and there in frantic haste she demanded Balcom's number.

It was some moments before Central could make the connection, and then it was only to Zita's disappointment and growing fear. The Madagascan servant of Balcom answered in the absence of his master.

"Is Mr. Balcom there?" asked Zita, adding, "Or Mr. Paul?"

The black shook his head. "Neither Mr. Balcom nor Mr. Paul is at home," he replied.

Zita was now thoroughly alarmed. Had she some connection with the Automaton? Or was it her fear that either Balcom or Paul might know more than they would care to have the authorities know? Or was the Automaton really an iron monster, after all?

That and many other questions were surging through the minds of all who had encountered this unique mystery.

CHAPTER XI

It was midnight when, far down in the rock-hewn cavern in which the Automaton had his secret den, the steel monster and one of his men stalked out through the arched passage that led to the very cellar of the house above them.

A few moments later the swinging rock door in the Grave-yard of Genius tilted and the two entered the strong-room, passing across the room and out through the steel door into the cellar. Up the cellar steps they proceeded until they reached the hall, then noiselessly they crossed into the library. With his human companion the monster approached the safe deliberately. Just as deliberately the Automaton reached out to turn the handle of the combination.

There was a flash as the current passed through the arm of steel to the foot of steel resting on the plate Locke had set in the floor. A suppressed cry escaped from the henchman. As for the monster, he strove with superhuman force to wrench himself away from the electric trap.

Meanwhile, up in his laboratory in the house, Locke and four men from the Department of Justice had been waiting.

"The Department expects us to get this evidence *right*," he had emphasized as he gave them their instructions.

Hardly had he finished when a signal light which Locke had arranged on the wall flashed, giving the information that the trap had worked.

Out of the laboratory all piled, running down the hall, Locke paused only a second to tap on Eva's door, as she had asked, if anything happened, so that she might be present at the capture. An instant and Eva, too, had joined the pursuit.

Down in the library the Automaton struggled with the current. As the rug was kicked aside, the emissary saw the wire from the plate and quickly traced it to its source.

The result was that in a few seconds the emissary had found a wall switch and pulled it. Instantly the Automaton was released from the power that held him.

Quickly the man of steel raised and lowered his arms, as though to be sure that he could do so, at the same time indicating orders to his follower, who leaped to guard the entrance to the room. Then the Automaton turned to open the safe, making swift use of the remaining seconds before the alarm might bring interference.

In almost no time he had the safe open, reached in, and seized a packet of precious papers, apparently. Then he turned and was gone, regardless of the man whom he had sent to guard him.

In the hall, Locke's sharp ears had detected the approach of the emissary. Not knowing whether it might be the villain himself, he cautioned the men to wait an instant. The emissary, coming along, crouching and listening, did not see Locke, and thus Locke was able to seize him and with a spectacular throw project him literally into the hands of the law in the person of one of his own men, who snapped the bracelets on the astonished thug as Locke, followed by Eva and the rest, ran on to the library.

No one was in the library as Locke ran in and looked about. He turned toward the door to the hallway where the portieres were drawn. As he was standing there, looking about, the portieres moved behind him. Suddenly they were jerked aside from their fastenings and flung over his head. As this happened, the ponderous hand of the Automaton descended on Locke's head and he sank to the floor as the portieres wrapped about him.

When the department agents with Eva arrived, they were merely in time to untangle Locke from the curtains. The Automaton had fled safely.

Although his head was still reeling from the blow, Locke started to question the prisoner, but gave it up as a bad job and hurried over to examine the safe, followed by Eva.

Their dismay was mutual. Not only was the safe door open, but the paper was gone.

Question the emissary as they would, they could get nothing out of him. Such men have keenly developed the gang instinct of silence. They would sooner die than squeal.

Even a night in jail failed to break the reticence of the emissary, although he had been subjected to the most strenuous third degree.

Not only had his spirit not been broken, but the fellow was keenly alert and planning a way to secure his own release.

As a prison guard was taking the emissary back to his cell, after a thorough quizzing by Locke in the warden's office, the emissary whispered:

"Want to make a piece of change—safe?"

The guard looked about, saw that the coast was clear to speak, but before he could do so the emissary spoke again.

"Give me a piece of paper and a pencil."

Quickly the thug scratched away at a note.

"Deliver that," he said to the guard, handing him the note he had written, "and you'll get something worth while."

The guard nodded as he shoved the thug into his cell and locked the door, then walked off, while the fellow watched eagerly through the bars.

Locke in the warden's office, unsuccessful in making the prisoner talk, had evolved another scheme.

"Put me in the cell next to him," decided Locke. "I have a plan."

It was while the false guard was reading the address on the note that Locke and the warden entered the cell row. The guard hastily stuffed the message in his pocket as Locke and the warden passed up toward the empty next cell.

Locke went through all the actions of one who was being thrown into a cell, and the emissary in his own cell listened without suspecting anything. Locke had arranged with the warden to leave the cell unlocked, but no sooner had the warden left than the guard, who had been observing, moved over and shot the bolts.

Here, then, was a predicament. Locke could not give the alarm without putting the emissary in the next cell on guard. Rapidly Locke revolved in his head scheme after

Arthur B. Reeve and John W. Grey

scheme. He was an expert on bolts and knew that at any moment he could release himself. Should he do so now? Instead he concluded to wait until the guard returned, for by the man's actions Locke was sure that something queer was going on, although, naturally, he did not know what it was. Accordingly Locke lay down on the bunk in the cell and decided to wait.

Some time later, at a deserted house not far from the rock-hewn den of the Automaton, the false prison guard might have been seen delivering the message which the prisoner had written to two other emissaries of the Automaton.

After a hasty conference they decided on their course of action. Not only did he receive the money the prisoner had promised him, but the emissaries gave him minute instructions regarding the rescue which they planned. A cap and a pair of goggles for the prisoner were given to the guard and he was sent on his way.

Scarcely had he gone when the Automaton himself entered the deserted house, and under his direction one of the emissaries wrote a note which he addressed to Eva. For, with Locke out of the way, it was a splendid time to take advantage of the poor girl.

The note read simply: "Our prisoner has confessed. Meet me at the Cliff House at eight o'clock," and bore the signature of Locke.

Thus, with their plans carefully laid, the Automaton and his emissaries plotted, and soon a messenger was on his way to Eva with the faked message.

Meanwhile, as the day wore on, the treacherous guard returned on duty at the prison, and at the first opportunity made his way to the cell in which the emissary was locked.

In a hoarse whisper he told the fellow of the success of his mission and of the plan, slipping to him the cap and goggles through the bars.

Locke had been waiting for hours impatiently on his bunk, but now was all attention, though he was careful not to betray it. As the guard left and the emissary was trying on the cap and goggles, Locke came to his cell door. Now was the time to act.

He began working noiselessly and swiftly with the bolts, deftly determining just how the tumblers fell until he was able to slip the bolt. He peered into the next cell. The emissary had retired to his own bunk to await the time of rescue. Locke saw his chance, and at once began unlocking the cell door. As the emissary heard him, he concluded that it was the guard come to release him, and sprang from his bunk just as Locke entered. He suspected nothing until a stray ray of light fell on Locke's face. But then it was too late either for him to put up much of a fight or to make an outcry. For with a swift blow Locke disposed of him and carried the fellow, unconscious, into his own cell, where he locked the door again, hurrying back to the emissary's cell, where he donned the fellow's clothes, of which he had stripped him, and appropriated the cap and goggles. Then Locke waited for the rescue that was to lead, he was sure, straight to the villains he wished to capture.

At Brent Rock, the faked telegram from Locke had been delivered and Eva was overjoyed to learn of his seeming success. As it happened, Zita was in the library when the butler brought the message in, and, all animation, was eager to accompany Eva to the meeting-place. But Eva would not listen to it.

So, not many moments before eight that night, while Locke was waiting in the jail for the rescuers, Eva climbed into her

Arthur B. Reeve and John W. Grey

speedster, eager to keep the appointment which she was convinced would clear up the mystery.

In the darkness outside the jail, by this time, was waiting the false turnkey when an open car drove up with its motor silenced. He had been expecting it and so was ready when a heavily goggled man climbed out and signaled to him. In the back of the car was another man, also goggled, while the chauffeur, alone, had his face also well hidden by a cap over his eyes and his collar pulled up.

Understanding perfectly, the guard hurried into the jail, making sure that the coast was clear, and down the cell row to the cell where Locke was waiting impatiently, now dressed and hunched up in a perfect imitation of the emissary. The turnkey opened the door and whispered to Locke, who nodded gruffly, and together they sneaked quietly out.

With scarcely another word, outside, Locke leaped into the waiting car and the four were off, leaving the false turnkey chuckling over his cleverness and ready to make a get-away.

Locke glanced furtively from the driver to the other two passengers in the car as it sped along in the direction of the cliffs. So far everything had gone fine. When would they begin to suspect the substitution he had played on them? He revolved rapidly in his mind just what he would do under various circumstances.

"Well, old pal," exclaimed one, clapping him on the shoulders, "how does it seem to be out?"

Locke replied with gruff heartiness, and the others now began to remove their goggles. Locke, however, did not do the same. They exchanged a glance.

Already Eva had arrived at the Cliff House, had left her car, and was approaching on foot, just as Locke with the now thoroughly aroused emissaries swung into sight.

With a shout to the driver, the two in the back of the car leaped at Locke at once, and, as the car stopped, the chauffeur joined them.

Even prepared as he was, Locke was no match for three of them, and, fighting furiously, all four combatants rolled over and over as they came closer to the door of an old acid-mill that adjoined the Cliff House.

"We must keep him from saving the girl," panted the leader of the emissaries to the others.

Inside the old building stood some huge tanks of acid, and as they rolled nearer and nearer to them it became evident that Locke was in their power.

Suddenly one emissary reached out and secured a coil of rope, which he unwound quickly. The others, too, saw their chance. It was fiendish. Round and round they wound the rope until they had Locke well-nigh helpless. Then one of them cast the end of the coil over a beam, all seized the end as it fell on the other side, and Locke found himself dangling head downward from the beam, suspended over the vat of acid.

They were about to drop him into it when one, more alert and more fiendish than the rest, cried out, "Look!"

Through a window now they could see Eva, and back of her the terrible figure of the Automaton, stalking. She had walked directly into the trap, but the fight with Locke had delayed the emissaries. Wildly now Eva was running over the lawn, full in the direction of the acid-room from the

Cliff House.

"Quick!" directed the emissary. "She'll come in that door. Fasten the rope on it. Then his own sweetheart will drop him into the acid!"

It was only a matter of seconds, as the screams of Eva came closer and closer, for the emissaries to carry the rope and jam it into the door through which pretty soon Eva would run to take refuge from the pursuing Automaton. Then they slunk back through a rear door, with muttered taunts to Locke, who struggled in the tangle of rope as he felt the stinging fumes of the acid below.

Outside, Eva, who had realized at last that it was a trap and had no thought that Locke might be anywhere about, fled toward the acid-room, while the emissaries hid, ready to seize her as she opened the door which was to plunge her lover into a horrible death in the acid seething below him.

CHAPTER XII

Locke's case seemed at last hopeless. The cruel ropes bit into his flesh and increased his agony, while the acrid fumes from the seething acid were slowly stupefying that keen brain of his.

Backward and forward like a huge pendulum his body swayed, and in an agony of suspense he watched the fatal rope. With writhing body he swayed far out, and then he saw just one chance.

The emissaries had thrown the rope over a beam which was far above Locke, and it seemed an impossibility for him to reach it. For one less resourceful or with a physique less perfectly developed, even to try would have been useless. But there was one chance in a thousand, and he grasped it eagerly.

Alternately contracting and relaxing his muscles, Locke succeeded in swinging himself in an ever-widening arc. Nearer he swung—back—and again nearer. Could he make it? Back again and a terrific effort. He was gaining.

There came to him the sound of running feet. In his fear and agony he could have shrieked, but from his parched throat there issued no sound. Friend or foe, for him it meant the same fate—one touch on that knob and a

Arthur B. Reeve and John W. Grey

torturing death by fire.

With bursting muscles he redoubled his efforts. In a long sweep his body swayed out and up. Would he be in time? Those pattering feet, they were coming nearer and nearer. There were now but a few yards between them and that knob.

A mighty swing, a monstrous heave, his fingers crooked talon-like, and he touched the rafter, clutched—and missed.

Downward and backward, his mind now reeling in black despair. He had tried and failed. This was the end. The sound of footsteps had ceased. Well he knew that some one was at the door. He tried to pray and then—he crashed against the rafter. Mechanically he grasped at it and clung.

The door flew open, and there stood Eva. All the horrors of imminent death, even the pain of sorely tried muscles, were momentarily forgotten in his relief at seeing her safe and having saved himself. But not yet was he free. The emissaries had been thorough in their work, but it was not many moments before the last knot was loose and he dropped to the floor.

Locke peered stealthily about. To all appearances everything was clear. He placed his arm about Eva and they started to steal out. Well they knew that, with such enemies, not for a moment would they dare relax their caution. For them every angle and nook was a temporary haven. Slowly they drew away from the dread spot, and soon came to a more populous locality where the lights of honest shops and peaceful homes gave them a sense of greater security and brought a feeling of unreality to the horrors through which they had passed.

A taxi-driver hailed them, and in a short time they were

rolling along the Cliff Drive and had arrived at Brent Rock.

It was the following day that the old butler handed Locke a letter addressed to International Patents, Incorporated, from the Diving and Salvage Company. Locke was about to read it, when Eva entered and they read it together.

"We are reliably informed," read the letter, "that the Under Seas Corporation is trying to obtain possession of the self-liberating diving-suit which you control in our interest. This must be prevented."

Locke was immediately interested. At once it occurred to him that here was a patent which the company had suppressed which might prove of incalculable value.

"This suit might be very valuable to the government," he exclaimed to Eva. "I am going to try it myself."

"Please don't," pleaded Eva. "It isn't worth it. It's not worth the risk."

Locke, however, realized that here was something of extreme importance, and as he visualized to Eva the helplessness of a deep-sea diver, his air-line cut, struggling in vain to release himself and rise to the surface, he began to win her over.

At the moment when Quentin and Eva were in the library, Zita was taking advantage and was ransacking Locke's laboratory, not with any definite purpose in mind, but searching in every nook for some clue which might tell her what he was about.

The speed with which she worked was extraordinary. Yet, before she moved an instrument, a retort, a book, its position was minutely studied, so that she could restore it to its former place without any one suspecting that it had ever

Arthur B. Reeve and John W. Grey

been moved.

It was while she was thus occupied that her eye fell upon an instrument which aroused in her an excited interest. It was very like the headpiece used by operators of telephones, and she hastened to adjust it. In a moment it was as though she were in the library. She could hear Locke's earnest laugh and in it Zita could detect an undercurrent of tenderness. Her lips compressed and her eyes hardened as she listened. Locke was speaking about a letter and it seemed to be something important. Zita was all ears.

But Locke's next words which she heard were his decision to test the diving-suit, and as she listened she became tense, for this information she knew was important. The continued note of tenderness in Locke's voice more infuriated Zita. She removed the headpiece of the dictagraph, slammed it back into the desk drawer from which she had taken it, and hurried out.

In the library, Locke, having persuaded Eva, left her and went down into the Graveyard of Genius, where he touched the secret spring and the massive door flew open. He entered the gloomy place and went at once to the shelf upon which lay the self-liberating diving-suit. He took the suit down and examined its every detail minutely. As he did so he became more and more enthusiastic and he could find no fault with any of its features.

"It's entirely practical," he exclaimed to himself. "I'm going to try it to-day."

He closed the great door and remounted the stairs, carrying the suit with him. But had he noticed the fiery eyes that had watched him through the secret rock door of the cavern he would not have been so eager to try the test he had in mind.

By this time Eva had called her car, and together Locke and Eva drove to the near-by cove, where there was a little launch which he planned to use.

Out into the river they sailed, Eva at the wheel, while Locke busied himself over the sputtering engine. Soon they arrived at a spot which was suitable for the test of the suit.

Locke had brought along the full equipment, and, while Eva took charge of the air-pump, Locke donned the diving-suit. Soon all was ready and Locke descended over the side, after carefully instructing Eva in each detail. Eva started pumping, while with her other hand she carefully paid out the air-line and signal-cord.

But in their close attention to the task in hand, neither had noticed a low, knifelike launch that had followed them and that was now hovering a short distance off.

Locke was now walking over the shell-strewn bottom, examining curious objects here and there. The tide was setting in strongly and at times it was with difficulty that he kept his feet.

He had become satisfied that this particular suit filled all the requirements of a first-class diving-suit, and he was about to try its special, self-liberating feature, when his attention was arrested by a vague mass which seemingly moved against the current.

This was so extraordinary that his first thought was of a shark. He stopped in his tracks and became motionless, for it is a well-known fact that these sea tigers rarely see an object unless it is in motion. Still, the vague form slowly took on more distinctness as in its course it gradually drew nearer to him. It was then that Locke was almost overcome with surprise. For there, groping his way toward him, was a diver, like himself.

What was this strange being doing there on the bottom of the sea? Whence had he come? Locke could not guess. For, like Eva, he had not noticed the other launch. It seemed impossible to him. Still, to him, apart from curiosity at the appearance of the other diver, the incident had no other interest. What had he to fear from any man at the bottom of a peaceful harbor? Locke moved nearer.

The stranger allowed him to approach, stopped, even, as though he were himself amazed at Locke's appearance, and Locke made gestures to reassure the man of his good intentions.

Locke was quite close now, and through the glass gate in the other's helmet he could see his eyes. But in those eyes he could see no responding friendliness. There was a murderous hate instead. He tried to step back and place himself in a position for defense, but he was too late. For, with a movement amazingly rapid for one under water, the stranger leaped upon him, at the same time drawing a long knife. There, under the sea, commenced a battle royal.

Locke was unarmed and so from the start was at a disadvantage. The stranger seemed not so anxious to stab him as to come to close quarters, and before Locke could prevent him he had done so. With his left hand he grabbed Locke's lines, while with the other, in which was the keen knife, he slashed murderously.

Locke tried to break his grip. But the other was not to be denied. With one stroke he cut through both lines, pushing Locke backward and himself springing free at the same time.

Immediately Locke's helmet filled with sea water, while the pressure became enormous. Locke tried to hold his breath, while his hand searched for the liberating knob. He gave it one twist. It worked perfectly. Locke's suit, including the helmet, simply opened and fell from him.

Propelled as much by the pressure that the water exerted as by his own powerful strokes, Locke shot to the surface.

The day was perfect and the bay was calm. For a few seconds Locke floated, drawing the air into his starving lungs. Then he raised himself and gazed about him. At first glance everything seemed the same except for the fact that, whereas before his own boat had been alone, there were now two. Then Locke heard an agonizing call for help—from Eva.

After he had gone over the side of their launch Eva was naturally very intent upon keeping him plentifully supplied with air. He had been down some time before, glancing about, she had spied the other launch. But at the time she had thought little of it. For her, all thought of danger was centered on the man who was now risking his life many fathoms beneath her from pure motives of patriotism.

It was only, some minutes later, when she heard the grating of another boat against the side of her own that she realized that she herself stood in danger. But even at that moment her thoughts were of Quentin, who now for the first time was wholly dependent on her efforts alone. She looked up fearfully, and what she saw fairly congealed the blood in her veins. Directing a murderous emissary to board Eva's launch, in the cockpit of the other boat stood the Automaton!

Not for an instant did Eva cease her efforts at the pump. But she shrieked with terror again and again. Now, to add to that terror, the pressure on the air-pump suddenly ceased. From the depths myriads of bubbles of air arose.

Knife in hand, the emissary leaped aboard and came toward her. Automatically, frantically, she still turned the useless pump, while with her free arm she tried to ward off the poised knife.

Again her shriek for help echoed across the water—and this time her call was answered.

Had she gone mad? The voice that answered her was the voice of the man she loved. Her brain reeled and she fell at the feet of the murderous thug.

Other cries, then shouts were now heard, for some fisher folk were putting out off shore to discover what all the tumult was about.

The Automaton made a hasty gesture to the emissary, who sprang back from his victim and leaped to his own launch, where, with his assistance, there was barely time to haul aboard the chief thug, who had been sent below to attack Locke. The launch cast off and with ever-increasing speed headed down the river.

Locke was the first to arrive and climb over the side of the boat. Dripping though he was, he took Eva in his arms and bathed her face, while by this time other craft arrived and friendly hands did all they could to care for them both.

It was some minutes before Eva was restored and all headed again to the shore, eager to help Locke.

As he assisted Eva to land, and they waited for a carriage, Locke hastily offered a boatman a liberal reward for the discovery of the precious diving-suit, for it had been his intention to present the patent to the government.

Meanwhile some strange things had happened. Paul and his

father had quarreled over money, over De Luxe Dora, over Paul's manner of life and his ill luck in winning Eva's affections.

At the same time Dora had become more insistent in her demands for money to meet her extravagances, and Paul conceived an idea of selling one of the patents to a rival company. Strange to say, it had been the self-liberating diving-suit and the rival company was the Under Seas Company.

All this took place some time after the disappearance of the Automaton and his precious crew.

Some hours later that evening a telephone message came for Locke from the boatman that the diving-suit had been recovered and was being held by him.

Locke replied that he would be down in an hour. But during that hour other strange things occurred. For no sooner had the boatman hung up his receiver than a pleasant voice hailed him and he left his house to investigate. It was Paul Balcom.

It was in a clever, insinuating, affable manner that Paul approached the real object of his visit. His appeal was cleverly worded, cleverly presented. The sole object was to awaken the poor boatman's cupidity.

The sum mentioned, no less a sum than five thousand dollars, would mean luxury to the poor man. And all for what? Simply to call up a stranger, a Mr. Locke, to tell him that the boatman demanded more money since he had telephoned before, that the cash was to be placed by him in an old packing-case from which a stationary engine had been removed that morning. It was just an exchange. That was all.

"Sure I'll do that," the boatman told Paul, and Paul, smiling craftily, gave him his hand to seal the bargain.

The boatman went back to his quarters and again called Brent Rock, making his new demands. Locke was tremendously indignant, but he wanted the suit quickly to prevent its falling into unscrupulous hands. He agreed and immediately started for the dock.

The boatman turned from his telephone and, picking up the suit, regarded it curiously. "Five thousand dollars," he muttered. "Five thousand dollars." And he shook his head wonderingly.

He was standing near an open window and was commencing to fold the suit preparatory to taking it to the end of the dock where lay the engine-case, when, without the slightest warning, three emissaries of the Automaton, who had appeared just a moment before on the dock, leaped through the window and felled him to the floor. He struggled feebly, but it was no use, and a final blow left him unconscious.

The emissaries next grabbed the diving-suit and left hurriedly by the way they had come. But they had not completed what it was they sought to do.

The old boatman was not as badly hurt as it seemed and was able to drag himself across the floor with just strength enough to pull the telephone from the table and call Brent Rock. Then as weakness again overcame him he managed to blurt out a message to Eva, who answered.

"Don't let Mr. Locke come to the dock," he managed to gasp. "He'll be killed." Then he collapsed and fainted.

Eva tried frantically to get the boatman again on the wire,

but it was useless. Quickly a plan formed in her mind.

If she could only intercept Locke before he reached the dock!

She dashed out to the garage, realizing that it was almost hopeless, since Locke had been gone some time. Hoping against hope, she jumped into her speedster and swung out and down the road.

The fact was that even as she sped along toward the cove Locke was passing the arched gate of the dock.

He called at the boatman's little shack. Of course there was no reply. To all appearances it was deserted. Thinking to find him at the very end of the dock where he had been told to place the money, he proceeded to the engine-case.

He was slightly surprised at not finding the boatman there, but as that was no part of the agreement it engaged his attention for only a moment. He started to withdraw the money from his pocket, groping at the same time to see if the diving-suit was actually in the case.

He was bending over when suddenly there was a rush of men behind him and a blackjack in the hands of one of the ruffians just missed his head.

He fought, but their numbers were overwhelming. Like a pack of wolves they pulled him down.

Locke was quickly bound with ropes and forced into the engine-case. The cover was put on and they nailed it down solidly. To make it doubly sure this time the case was then lashed with ropes and they were knotted.

Next the emissaries carried the case to a sloping landing

stage, preparatory to casting it into the river.

It was at this moment that Eva came running down the dock in wild search to intercept Locke. Wide-eyed, in the moonlight, she paused at what she saw.

The emissaries had given the packing-case its final shove. Scraping, it slid down the incline and toppled overboard. There was a great splash as it struck the water and immediately began to sink in the depths.

The engine exhaust had evidently protruded from the case, as there was a hole in its side slightly larger than a man's hand. To Eva's horror, though she had half expected it, she saw actually a hand thrust forth from this hole as if waving frantically.

The box sank lower as it rapidly filled with water.

Eva knew not what to do. Instinctively she knew that it was Locke. It was as though he had waved a last farewell.

Only the hand now showed above the surface. Finally that, too, disappeared beneath the waves.

Despairingly she turned to see if there was anything on the dock with which she might help Locke—and she saw the Automaton himself advancing from the shore toward her. She turned. The emissaries on the other end of the dock cut off any chance in that direction.

Without a moment's hesitation Eva poised herself a moment on the edge of the dock and leaped far out into the blackness of the river.

CHAPTER XIII

The box that held Locke a prisoner was now undoubtedly resting on the slimy bottom. Eva had totally disappeared. The Automaton, convinced that at last he had rid himself of his victims, waved away the emissaries and departed.

Except for the tiny lights of ships on the river and the staccato exhaust of a tugboat, the river flowed with nothing to remind one of the two tragedies of only a few seconds ago.

As far as the eye could see, the surface of the water was unbroken. Then, suddenly, the scene changed. For from out the water, as though hurled up by a catapult, shot a man's body.

It was Locke.

By what miracle had he escaped from the watery grave?

From the time he was a small boy the study of locks and bolts, of knots and strait-jackets, of anything that could restrain or bind a man, had held a marvelous fascination for him, until now he was recognized as one of the world's greatest experts on these subjects. The great lock concerns often sent for him to test new inventions, and invariably he could point to any flaw in the constructions of them that existed. As he came to manhood his knowledge had grown apace until to many he seemed a veritable sorcerer.

It was by a trick known only to himself that he had been able to extricate himself from his desperate plight at the river's bottom. True, his flesh was lacerated. True, he was on the verge of total collapse. But he lived.

He made his way slowly toward the dock and was resting against one of the piles when he heard a faint cry. He strained his ears to locate the direction whence it came. Once again that feeble call floated across the water, and in it there sounded something vaguely familiar.

He was more rested now and he swam farther under the dock. Again came the cry. With a thrill now he recognized the voice.

"Eva!" he called, again and again.

"Here I am," came back the echo.

With a powerful stroke he breasted the current and in a moment he was supporting her half-fainting body. Precarious though their position was, Locke felt the thrill of her words. The effect was to spur him on to fresh efforts.

Eva had become stronger now. For a few moments he swam, in order, if possible, to find some means by which they might escape from the water and reach the dock.

They had no way of knowing but that the Automaton and his emissaries might still be lurking above, ready to thrust them back into the water or to reserve for them some even more terrible fate. But it was a risk that they realized must be taken and at once. An attempt to swim to another dock could end only disastrously.

Locke soon returned with the cheering news that he had discovered a ladder that came even to the surface of the water, a landing for small boats. More than that, he had mounted the ladder, and from a short survey he had seen no sign of their enemies.

Carefully aiding Eva, Locke swam to this ladder and soon they stood upon the dock, safe.

With great caution they moved toward the street and, without harm, finally passed beneath the arched gates again and were in the city street.

Eva went at once to her father's room. His condition was one of great weakness. The laughing madness had abated in so far that the poor victim was so weak that the spasms could not maintain a very violent form.

Eva practised all those little kindnesses which are known only to women, and tears were in her eyes as she stroked his poor gray head.

How terrible was it that, after all they had attempted, all that they had suffered, they should still stand defeated in their aim to get the antidote that would cure her father's malady. However, the brave girl was not one to admit herself beaten, and even as she sat there she was planning new ways to discover who were her terrible adversaries and to bring defeat to them.

At Brent Rock the next morning an aged inventor named Winters arrived before Locke was down-stairs, and was shown into the library to wait.

Locke soon descended from the laboratory and went into the room to meet him. But Winters was so agitated that at first he could hardly speak. It was some moments before he

112   Arthur B. Reeve and John W. Grey

gained control.

"What can I do for you, sir?" inquired Locke, although he knew the man must be one wronged by the patents company.

"One of my inventions was returned to me, when I protested once," the man replied, "but nothing has been done about two others."

"Please try to have a little further patience," pleaded Locke. "Everything is being done to assure justice to all."

"But, Mr. Locke," the man persisted, "I must insist on the return or the immediate marketing of the two inventions now in the possession of International Patents or I will—"

He paused, for Eva had entered and was overhearing what Winters was demanding.

"I am sure that, as my father returned one of your inventions," she interrupted, "he would wish me to return the other two, and I shall do so at once. Mr. Locke, will you be so kind as to get them?"

Locke immediately left the room and descended to the Graveyard of Genius for the two models.

In the laboratory above were Balcom and Zita, for she had told him of her discovery of the dictagraph. Balcom had the headpiece firmly clamped over his head and was drinking in the purport of the conversation down in the library.

Zita was almost beside herself with curiosity, as Balcom repeated only scraps of the conversation that went on below, but finally the real subject of the whole matter was repeated to her and she was satisfied at last. A peculiar look came into her eyes. As for Balcom, one would have thought that a whole world's treasure had suddenly been placed within his grasp. Yet each was cautious not to betray too much to the other.

Over the dictagraph came the words spoken by Eva, "Mr. Locke and I will come to your workshop at eight this evening to complete the transaction."

Locke in the mean time had brought the two models into the library and the inventor had almost danced with joy at seeing the children of his brain again.

Sent down by Balcom, Zita had been ordered to spy on Eva and Locke. She had been nearly caught by Locke as he was returning from the Graveyard of Genius, but had slipped behind a pair of portieres at the end of the hall and had emerged only when Locke had entered the library. She had crept close to the door and was listening.

She, too, now heard the inventor exact a promise from Eva and Locke not to fail to be at his workshop at eight that night.

Zita had but a second to glide backward from the door as the inventor came out into the hallway where she stood. He gazed at her in such a strange, fixed manner that an uncanny feeling came over her. Then he passed out, just as Balcom came down the stairs.

"Why did that man look at me in such a strange manner?" she queried of Balcom.

A moment Balcom considered her, as though undecided to speak, then made up his mind.

"Because," he replied, slowly, "he knows the secret of your

birth, knows who you really are."

Zita had no further chance to question Balcom, for at this instant Eva and Locke, still carrying the inventions, were leaving the library. Locke turned down again toward the stairway leading to the Graveyard of Genius, while Eva, nodding pleasantly to Zita and Balcom, mounted the stairs leading to her father's room.

Zita turned questioningly again to Balcom.

"Half of everything that girl possesses rightfully belongs to you," he whispered.

Zita apparently did not understand. "What shall I do to obtain my rights?" she asked.

"Do as I say," returned Balcom, as he left quickly.

It was some hours later that in the dark corner of the Graveyard of Genius the huge rock slowly swung outward. There was a clanging and clanking of metal. Two fiery eyes gleamed through the aperture and out stalked the hideous monster, the Automaton. With strange ominousness it went directly to the two models which Locke had returned, took them, turned and went back through the great gap in the wall from which it had come. Again slowly the huge rock swung back into place.

Locke, with some sort of intuition, had deduced that young Paul Balcom by his very absence might have played a leading part in all the events in which both Eva and himself had been thwarted and almost killed. Accordingly he determined to find and trail Paul.

It was some time after the models had been stolen in his absence that, in a taxicab, Locke, having gone from place to place which he knew Paul frequented, at last caught sight of him leaving a dance-hall of very ill repute. Paul was just stepping into a car which whisked him off rapidly and Locke gave an order to his own driver to follow him.

They wove in and out of various streets and finally turned up the Drive, where, after a few minutes, Paul's car came to a stop before a palatial apartment-house and Paul alighted. Looking up and down the Drive and seeing nothing to cause him suspicion, Paul entered the house.

Locke carefully noted the address, then leaned back in his cab to await developments.

Paul was taken to the third floor and there was admitted to a gorgeous apartment.

"I thought you'd never get here," languidly greeted the feline De Luxe Dora.

She led him to a chaise-longue seductively, taking care, however, that he should see a pile of unpaid bills that lay upon a table near it.

Paul was not entirely at his ease and wasted no time in coming to the point.

"Look here, Dora," he began; "I know you can't run this shack on air. I got your note this morning. I've been busy and I've got an idea. I've made up my mind to take a couple of those inventions the company owns and sell them. It means coin."

Dora's eyes gleamed avariciously.

"Be patient," Paul added, "and I'll have you swimming in gold."

At this juncture three young fellows of the cabaret type, better known as "lounge lizards," were admitted to the apartment.

Paul cast a glance at Dora which clearly spelled jealousy and reproach. He knew the fellows. In fact, there were few denizens of the underworld whom he did not know. Concealing his vexation, he tried to greet them easily.

The fellows returned the salutation hastily.

"Say, Balcom," hastened one of them, "some one is on your trail, shadowing you."

Paul was startled and furious, but in this emergency it was Dora who thought out the plan of action.

"In a taxicab?" she repeated, as the others told what they had seen outside. "Listen to me, Paul. Go to the window and show yourself. Then leave the house. This fellow Locke will investigate—and we'll tend to the rest."

Paul moved to the window, opened it, and stepped out on a small balcony. Dora slipped to his side and for a moment they stood there gazing apparently at the view of the river. Then they re-entered the apartment.

"Now go, Paul," said Dora. "Whoever this fellow is, we'll handle him."

Paul started to get his hat, then stopped and from his pocket drew out a small package.

"I was going to use this elsewhere," he said, "but it might come in handy to—"

Dora reached for the package, but Paul withdrew it hastily.

"Careful, Dora," he admonished. "There's a small gas-bomb inside."

The five now conferred a bit and it was agreed that this time the inquisitive Mr. Locke would surely trouble them no more.

"With Locke out of the way," promised Paul to Dora, "the road to our fortune is clear."

A moment later Paul left the apartment, descended in the elevator, and jumped into a taxicab and was off.

Locke from his cab had, of course, seen all this, had seen Paul and Dora on the balcony and the departure. But he knew nothing of the three men who had gone to the same apartment.

He waited until Paul passed out of sight, then stepped out of his cab, making a careful calculation as to the exact location of the woman's apartment, for he had determined to find out about her. From the hall boy he learned that it was De Luxe Dora, of whom he knew, and it was only a matter of seconds when he was admitted.

Dora swept over graciously toward him.

"Will you answer me one question?" he asked, in answer to a query from her.

She nodded assent.

"How long have you known Mr. Balcom's son?"

"He is an old friend," she replied. "I'm expecting him to return at any moment. Won't you be seated? Please excuse me just a moment."

Before Locke could say a word she had left the room. Left alone himself, Locke took in all the details of the room and again and again his eye wandered to a Louis XIV desk.

Feeling certain that this woman was without doubt connected in some way with the plots, he felt justified in opening the desk to obtain evidence. He tiptoed over to it and tried to open it. It stuck at first, but after one or two silent, well-directed blows which he so well knew how to administer the sliding panel stood unlocked.

He glanced around. There was no one to be seen. He moved back the panel. There was a flash and a tiny puff of smoke. Locke coughed once, clutched at his throat, and lay gasping on the floor.

Immediately the three men rushed out, carrying ropes and holding handkerchiefs to their nostrils. One ran to the window and threw it wide open, admitting gusts of air to clear away the fumes. The others began to bind Locke as De Luxe Dora appeared in the doorway and calmly directed operations.

On the roof of the apartment several moments later in the just-gathering dusk five figures might have been seen. Three men and a woman were conferring, while at their feet was a man tightly bound and unconscious.

In the background was a huge water-tank, with a ladder leading to its brim.

Suddenly the conspirators straightened up. They had come to a decision. The three men lifted the unconscious figure and bore it up the ladder. The tank was empty. One of the men jumped down into it, while the others lowered their victim after him. Then they passed down ropes.

There were two spouts at the bottom of the tank through which water was pumped. Also there were pipes running upward. To these pipes they tied Locke. Then the men climbed out and, as their last fiendish act, turned the water on.

With a sneer Dora turned and led the way down-stairs again.

"They'll find his body when they have to clean the tank again," she exclaimed.

At Brent Rock, during the absence of Locke, Eva had donned her street clothes, since it was nearing the hour of eight when she and Locke were due to be at the inventor's workshop to render the restitution. She went down-stairs and asked the butler about Locke. But the man replied that Mr. Locke had not yet returned.

Eva was very uneasy by this time, and, thinking to save time, was about to go down to the Graveyard of Genius to get the models of the two inventions, when Zita came down the hall carrying a fair sized package which she tried hard to conceal. Eva greeted her and continued down to the cellar, as Zita, with a sort of grim smile, left the house.

Eva came to the great door, pushed the secret spring, and in a moment was inside the gloomy place. She went directly to the spot where the two inventions had been kept. They were gone.

Alarmed, she rushed up-stairs.

Still Locke did not return. Nor did any word come from him. It was now very near to eight. Eva decided to go, for surely Locke would be there.

Arthur B. Reeve and John W. Grey

When Zita arrived at the inventor's, in her hands was still the mysterious package. She carried it gingerly, then raised it to her ear. From within it there came a faint ticking sound. What was it inside?

She looked at her wrist-watch. It was still some minutes before eight. She knocked at the inventor's door.

The inventor at once admitted her. It was a neat little workshop in which every detail had been thought out with care—the home, one might say, of a methodical workman.

The inventor manifested some surprise at seeing Zita, but politely asked her to enter, and offered her a chair. Zita declined and plainly showed her nervousness.

"Will you please give this package to Mr. Locke and Miss Brent when they come at eight?" she asked.

Winters agreed and accepted the package, looking quizzically at her as he did so, just as he had earlier in the day.

Zita, unable to control her curiosity, burst out with the question uppermost on her mind.

"Why do you look at me in such a strange manner?" she queried.

The inventor merely turned his gaze away and shrugged.

"Mr Balcom tells me that you know the secret of my birth," pressed Zita.

The inventor looked up quickly. "Who did Mr. Balcom say you were?" he asked.

"He told me that I was Brent's daughter," replied Zita, keenly watching the aged face.

"Balcom lied to you," hastened the inventor.

Already there was a ponderous tread on the stairs, but Winters did not seem to notice it.

"You are not Brent's daughter," he pursued, more slowly.

The door opened swiftly and an emissary stood framed there, a knife poised in his hand. Behind him stood the Automaton.

"You are—"

At that instant the inventor caught sight of the intruders. With a look of horror in his eyes he threw out his hands to protect himself, but he was too late. The knife whizzed through the air and a second later pierced his throat. He fell to the floor—dead.

At the moment when the emissary, followed by the Automaton, entered, Zita, watching her chance, managed to escape from the room, stumbled, and almost half-fell down the stairs.

Already, in the huge water-tank that stood on the roof of the apartment of Dora, Locke had revived as he felt the water and had found himself already half submerged, with the water rapidly pouring in. At first he could not grasp his terrible predicament, but before long the full horror of it burst on him and he struggled madly to free himself. Since his body was stretched at full length, it was impossible to use the ordinary tricks of which he was master. His arms were bound, and he well knew that to release one of them constituted his sole chance of escape.

He contracted his muscles and, inch by inch, he worked his right arm free. By this time the water had risen until he was fairly beneath its surface. Could he last long enough to free himself?

He worked frantically. Finally, with his lungs almost bursting, he managed to free the other arm, then the rope that bound his neck. To release his feet was, to him, child's play, and he stood up.

But the water had risen almost to the top of the tank before he was able to grasp its brim and draw himself out.

Once on the roof, there was only one thought in his mind. It was nearing eight o'clock, and if Eva kept the appointment at the inventor's he knew his adversaries well enough to be sure that they would take advantage of his absence.

He dashed down the stairs and out of the building. Dora and her evil band could wait. He must reach the inventor's shop. As the seconds sped, so increased his premonition that all would not be well there.

It was at the moment that Zita came flying down-stairs that Locke burst into the hallway to the inventor's.

Zita saw him. Above, she knew was the terrible Automaton and his bloodthirsty emissary. More horrible yet, she had her fears of the package that had been given her by Balcom to deliver.

"You must not go up there!" she cried, impulsively, flinging her arms about Locke's neck.

Locke tried to remove her arms as he questioned her. But Zita either would not or could not tell more. Instead she merely clung to him.

Thus it was that Eva, determined at keeping her appointment with the inventor at all costs, entered the hallway at just this unpropitious moment. To her it looked as if Locke and Zita were very familiar. Could it be that Quentin was such a cad? She could not deny the evidence of her eyes.

Indignantly she brushed past them and rushed up the stairs. Locke called after her, but she refused to heed him. He flung off the arms of Zita and dashed after her. But Eva was too quick for him. She opened the door to the inventor's and went in, slamming it behind her. The lock snapped. In an instant Eva saw what she had fled into. There was the Automaton, near him the emissary with the knife—and on the floor their victim in a pool of blood. She shrieked and tried to escape. But the lock had snapped. Besides, the emissary, now directed by the monster, blocked her retreat.

Outside, Locke pounded on the door, but could not open it. It was of stout oak and would take some moments to break down.

The emissary circled in one direction. Eva turned, and there was the Automaton advancing on her from the other side of the room.

On the table the clock-work bomb, delivered by Zita, whether with full knowledge or not, ticked out the last few seconds before its timing at precisely eight!

CHAPTER XIV

Eva flattened herself against the door at her back. She could feel and hear Locke pounding on the other side. She thought that she would die of sheer terror.

The Automaton raised his mighty fist, and Eva instinctively ducked under the monster's arm. There was an inner room. Could she reach it in time? Would the door be unlocked? At most she could only try.

The emissary tried to catch her, but she proved too quick for him. She reached the door. It opened, and she flew into the room, slamming and bolting it behind her.

Now she could hear the thunderous blows of the Automaton raining against the door. One huge fist of the monster crashed through the panel. Eva crouched down in a far corner and closed her eyes. At that instant the time bomb exploded and the house was rocked to its foundations.

Everything was demolished. One entire side of the house was blown out. The door leading to the workshop which a moment before Locke had been vainly striving to open crashed full upon him and felled him, half-stunned, to the floor.

The force of the explosion had dazed Eva. As for the Automaton and the emissary, they had both been blown through a gaping aperture in the wall to land in the garden beneath. Only Zita, in the lower hallway, was totally untouched by the catastrophe.

Locke, dazed, crawled from under the door and made his way into the demolished room in search of Eva, a cold fear gripping his heart. How could any living thing have lived after such an occurrence? But in another instant he saw her, as she half swooned and staggered into the room.

"Quentin!" she gasped.

He caught her in his arms. But the next moment she remembered what she had witnessed in the hallway below and she drew herself away from him.

"Go to the girl you really love," she scorned.

"The girl—I really love?" repeated Locke; then there ran through his mind what had happened, as though it had been ages ago.

He protested and tried to explain. But protestations and explanations only made matters worse, as usual. Had she not with her own eyes seen Locke in Zita's arms?

"Eva," he persisted, manlike, "I swear that she was only trying to save my life. I cannot help it if she—"

Locke saw that his defense was only making an innocent matter worse, and checked himself. His mind recalled that some one had once said that a jealous woman believes a man guilty until he proves himself innocent; when he has proved himself innocent she merely still suspects. Eva's manner was very constrained.

At that moment a policeman, followed by Zita, entered, and Zita, running up to Locke, cried, anxiously, "You're not hurt—are you?"

Locke answered in an annoyed negative.

The policeman now questioned them very closely and examined the dead inventor's body. Then he entered their names and addresses in his note-book.

Next the officer lead the entire group down to the garden. There the horribly injured emissary was trying miserably to crawl away.

The Automaton had totally disappeared.

Eva immediately ordered that the injured man be taken to Brent Rock in her car. Then she turned sharply to Zita.

"How did you come to be here?" she demanded.

Zita was startled and confused. It lasted only a minute. Then, her mind made up, she replied, defiantly:

"I came here to discover the secret of my birth. I have been told that I am Mr. Brent's daughter."

Eva was stricken dumb with astonishment at this startling claim, but Locke laughed outright.

"What nonsense!" he scoffed. "Eva, don't listen to it."

Zita glared at him and with a haughty nod to Eva swept out of the garden.

Eva was still frightfully indignant with Locke and insisted on going home alone. However, they arrived at Brent Rock at about the same time.

The emissary had been placed on a lounge in the library and a doctor was called. The case was quite hopeless and they merely hoped to obtain a confession before he passed away.

When Eva arrived she went directly to her father's room, but, as he was receiving every attention from a trained nurse and she could do nothing further to aid him, she returned to the library.

Locke, too, after changing his clothes, still wet from the water-tank on the top of the apartment, also went to the library.

At his entrance the doctor glanced at him in a manner to indicate that there was no hope of saving the man's life. Locke went over to examine him. He was struck by the sly rascality of the professional criminal, but he thought little of it at the time. He tried to question the emissary, but, except for a labored breathing, could extract no response.

There were voices in the hallway. For a moment the dying man showed some signs of returning consciousness. A crafty look came over his face. What was he contemplating?

The door opened and Balcom and his son Paul entered. Balcom walked jauntily, but with a suavity of manner that was always his. Paul looked at his best, except for the fact that he carried his left arm in a silken sling.

Balcom greeted them all, and at his voice the dying man actually showed a sort of agitation. A strong shudder seemed to pass through his body, then, like a spring suddenly uncoiled, he sat up.

He was fully conscious now and strove to rise to his feet. It was a tremendous effort, but he succeeded, and stood confronting Balcom, while the ominous light of hatred that gleamed from his eyes as they encountered those of Balcom made even that well-poised man recoil and shudder.

With the muscles of his face working convulsively the dying thug tried to speak. All those standing in the library realized that it was to accuse, to denouce.

However, the effort proved too great, and with a groan that was ghastly the man fell backward on the couch, dead.

Murdering brute that he had been, still to Eva and Locke he now represented nothing but a stricken human being, with a human soul, blackened and warped. But Balcom and Paul seemed to show unmistakable signs of joy and relief. It was so evident, Locke thought, that he turned to them.

"Your coming seemed to have an unfortunate effect," he hinted. "The man seemed to know one of you—at least."

"Nothing of the kind," retorted Balcom, nettled.

Locke turned to Paul and regarded his injured arm questioningly. Paul, however, never lost his accustomed aplomb.

"I was hurt in an automobile accident," he explained, though with what seemed to be a trifle of nervousness.

Locke turned to the doctor. He was rubbing his hands, and smiling, with great unction, an action very unbecoming, to say the least, in a medical man who had just lost a patient. Taken all in all, Locke felt he could now sense the web of conspiracy tightening around him. The cards were still in the hands of his enemies.

He determined to incur any risk, to leave no stone unturned in order to bring the criminal to justice, whoever he might be. One thing encouraged him. The events seemed to have mollified Eva. He made an almost imperceptible signal to Eva, who left the room to dress for the street.

Meanwhile Locke left the library and went to a private telephone that connected the garage to the house. He ordered the chauffeur to have a fast runabout ready for instant call. Then, at the other telephone, he notified the coroner's office of the death of the emissary.

By this time Balcom, Paul, and the doctor came out of the library, the doctor in high good humor, for had he not received a huge fee? He left in his car.

Balcom and Paul, however, were slower in going, and paced the hallway in earnest conversation. Once they came to a dead halt close to the stairway leading down to the Graveyard of Genius. They listened intently. Evidently they came to a decision on something, for they left the house very hurriedly.

Immediately Locke called for the runabout. Eva came running down-stairs and in a moment they took up the trail of the Balcom car.

It seemed as if they traveled for miles, and Locke was commencing to think that it was merely a wild-goose chase, when Balcom's car came to a halt in one of the lower quarters of the city, before a house that was apparently tenantless.

To avoid discovery, Locke backed his car around a corner, got out, and watched their movements from a safe distance.

He saw Balcom, senior, alight, but Paul did not leave the

car. Locke was in some quandary what to do. To attempt to enter the house without Paul's seeing him and raising the alarm would, he realized, be impossible. Therefore he waited for nearly half an hour before his patience was rewarded by seeing Balcom come out of the house, jump into the car, and drive off hurriedly with Paul.

Locke walked to the house and looked closely over the exterior. It was little different from others in the same street. Then he walked thoughtfully back to Eva and they argued pro and con about the advisability of attempting to enter.

Locke insisted on entering alone, but Eva would not hear of it. Therefore, it was decided that they would go in together.

When Balcom had alighted from his car half an hour before he had merely stood for a moment in front of the door of the house when, mysteriously, the door had opened.

There was no one in sight. But he was so familiar with the house that it might have been his own. He descended a flight of stairs and stood before another door, where the same door-opening process was repeated.

Balcom entered a darkened room and for a moment seemed quite alone. Then from out the shadows, with a little half run, half lope, a strange figure of man came toward him.

He was in reality large of frame, but stooped and bent with age. An old frock-coat was wrapped about him. But the most remarkable things about the man were a pair of weirdly fascinating eyes with a mad glint in them and an enormous full beard, snow white, that fell almost to his waist.

At times the man talked rationally, in fact with the forcefulness of a great savant. Then, abruptly, he would leave off and the rest of his conversation was that of a babbling child. He was seldom at rest, scampering here and there, not unlike a bird-dog on a fresh scent. Seeking—always seeking—what?

Balcom grasped his arm in order to arrest his attention.

"Doctor Q," he addressed him, "you can have the revenge you have sought so long. Have you prepared everything?"

The old man chuckled and wagged his head in senile fashion. Balcom grabbed both his shoulders so that the old man was facing him, and shook him slightly.

"Your enemies are here," he emphasized. "Have you prepared for their reception?"

And then the haze beclouding the old man's brain seemed to pass away and his next moments were lucid.

"Ah, it's you, Balcom. You were just saying—"

Balcom explained that Locke and Eva had tracked him and on his departure would undoubtedly enter to investigate the place. Doctor Q, for such was his odd name, understood now, and an evil grimace distorted his wrinkled face.

"Let them come," he growled. "I am prepared. Why, I have even improved certain features of the Chair of Death."

He led Balcom into an inner room where many electric bulbs were dimly glowing. At their entrance two brutal-looking men straightened up from their task and saluted Balcom with great deference. Then they resumed their tasks as electricians.

"Want to see her work, sir?" one of the pair asked.

Stepping around a partition that separated the knife-switch from the room in which stood the electric chair, Balcom watched.

The chair was of practically the same construction as the chairs used in prisons for the supreme penalty, with electrodes to connect at the head, arms, and legs of the man to be electrocuted.

"Stand back, sir," called one of the men as he shot the switch home.

Instantly a snapping sound was heard as the current surged through, and the crackling sound such as the now familiar wireless makes as the long sparks leap from pole to pole. It was Force.

A satisfied look came into Balcom's eyes and he warmly congratulated the mad inventor, who followed him to the door and watched him as he mounted the stairs to depart with his son.

Soon after the departure Doctor Q went to a strange-looking instrument that seemed to have many of the characteristics of the periscope. He pulled a lever, a panel opened, and immediately the space directly in front of his street door was revealed to him. He stood there, watching intently, much as a spider watches for a fly.

Soon Locke and Eva showed in the panel above. He next pressed a button and saw the two enter. Then he went to a huge divan on the other side of the room and whipped off a covering that was concealing some gigantic thing beneath.

It was the Automaton, prostrate, at full length, without motion. At least it seemed so.

The madman glanced around, and then glided into an inner room from the larger one. He was just in time, for a moment later Locke and Eva entered.

They, too, glanced around fearfully. They saw the dread form of the Automaton and, although it did not move, Locke would have admitted he was ready to beat a retreat.

It was uncanny, weird. In the dim light the monster seemed to assume gigantic proportions. But he lay so still that their jangling nerves became quieted. They even approached him, Locke with automatic in hand in case the iron terror were shamming. But there was no sign of life—or whatever it was that animated this thing.

Locke, handing his gun to Eva, determined to investigate further. He went to the inner door and listened. But he could hear no sound. He turned the knob and entered. He was amazed at what he saw. But, as there was apparently no living thing about, he took courage and entered farther. He took note of the switches, saw the deadly chair, and was about to test the apparatus to see if it could be possible that a practical electric chair existed in the heart of a peaceful city, when he heard Eva shriek in heart-rending terror.

He rushed madly back to where he had left her. But as he passed through the door some one dealt him a blow on the head, and as though pole-axed he dropped to the floor.

After Locke had left her to go into the inner room Eva's fears revived and she wished to follow him. But she was ashamed to have him think her a coward. She forced herself to remain rooted to the spot.

Her eyes had followed Locke through the doorway and her ears were strained to hear the faintest sound from the other room. In her anxiety about Locke's safety she even forgot the Automaton, and, in turning the better to watch the doorway, she drew nearer to the divan upon which the monster lay.

It was this action that had brought her into peril. Slowly one of the monster's arms commenced to move, and before Eva could spring away she was enfolded in his deadly embrace. It was that that made her shriek madly, wildly, in utter terror.

Then she saw Locke running through the door to her, saw him struck from behind, and she fainted.

The Automaton, evidently thinking Eva dead, let her limp body slip to the floor. For a moment it towered over her, as though contemplating whether to trample on her or no. At this juncture an emissary distracted its attention and the terror left her lying there without further injury.

The Automaton now assumed command of Locke's electrocution.

Under its direction the emissaries picked up Locke's body and placed it in the electric chair. They slit his trousers so that the deadly electrodes might form a better contact with his flesh. His sleeves were rolled back for the same reason. Next the headpiece was firmly adjusted. Now all the straps were tightly clinched.

The Automaton waved his arm.

A man stepped to the switch.

CHAPTER XV

There was a moan from the front room. Eva was recovering from her faint. The Automaton indicated to the emissary at the switch to do nothing until he had found out what was going on.

Locke had, meanwhile, recovered consciousness and realized his awful position. Here was a situation which, on its face, seemed unescapable. Yet Locke would not give in.

Straining every effort, he tried to extricate himself before the deadly current could sever the thread of life. Seconds seemed ages. Still he tried.

With a mighty effort he strained every muscle of his gigantic chest and the very straps that held him groaned from the force of his muscular exertion. Even now the death-man was at the switch and it was barely a question of seconds or heart-beats between him and death.

With a quick twist of his giant shoulder he threw his whole weight against the chest strap and it parted. Lurching forward, he freed his head and neck from the cruel straps, which snapped and parted.

The death-man paused for a fraction of a second to see what caused the commotion in the chair. To that pause Locke

Arthur B. Reeve and John W. Grey

owed his life. With a final supreme effort he threw himself on the floor just as the knife-switch swung into position and the wicked blue flame of death leaped across the head electrodes.

Once freed, he catapulted himself across the room and with a vicious upper-cut sent the emissary sprawling unconscious to the floor. Without a thought of himself he rushed into the next room where Eva now stood in panic, glued to the spot, in fear of the Frankenstein monster that would crush her in its grasp.

With murderous mien the thing crossed the room slowly, until only the table stood between her and destruction.

Like a wild animal Locke hurled himself into the room and with a master stroke of quick wit flung the heavy oaken table over at the monster. Then he seized Eva, and before the monster could turn in its tracks, half dragged, half carried her from the room.

In the hall further difficulty confronted Locke, for the place was well guarded. Several henchmen darted forth from dark corners of the murky place and would have intercepted him.

As the first approached, Locke, with a quick jiu-jitsu thrust, hurled him for a fall that would have broken the back of a less hardy man. The next one was just turning the top of the stairs, and Locke, quick to take advantage of the situation, adopted the only means of escape.

He seized the man bodily about the waist and, lifting him over his head, threw him upon his other oncoming foe. The result was that the two were flung down the stairs.

"Run!" he cried to Eva in a voice that was a command.

Without waiting he picked her up and carried her over the sprawling mass of legs and arms to safety below.

Once outside, he felt a little embarrassed at having the beautiful girl in his arms and he half murmured an apology as he placed her feet gently on the ground.

Life at Brent Rock was far from monotonous.

Like a great game of checkers, the various members of the establishment were being moved about, guided by some strange hand, it seemed.

Now one, then another seemed to gain the advantage, and as each strove for control of the vast fortune, the battle of wits surged back and forth.

Balcom was playing a game, it was plain. But to what extent? Sometimes it seemed as though Zita was his aide and would stop at nothing to succeed. Again it was that Zita played the game alone, still fostering her secret but hopeless love for Locke. Again it seemed as if Paul were playing the game, either alone or with some one else.

Just now it was apparent that Balcom and Zita, for their own ends, whatever might be the identity of the Automaton, planned a coup for themselves.

During one of Locke's absences Zita had secured access to his laboratory, and while looking around had discovered the dictagraph hidden in the desk drawer. Often Balcom and Zita, either together or alone, had taken advantage of the discovery.

It was at a time when both were using the mechanical eavesdropper on Locke and Eva in the library that Locke suddenly decided to return to the laboratory, without saying

Arthur B. Reeve and John W. Grey

anything about it.

Zita's quick ear heard him down the hall.

"Quick!" she warned. "Some one is coming!"

She sprang toward the closet door, which stood ajar, and in an instant Balcom was with her. The two were concealed in the closet as the laboratory door opened and Locke entered.

Locke walked to his table of test-tubes and picked up one containing mercury. What prompted this action he did not know. Perhaps it was his fascination for the elusive metal. Perhaps it was some subconscious feeling. At any rate, he held it aloft and gazed at it in the light. As he did so a strange thing happened. Reflected in its surface on the glass, yet distorted like a convex mirror, he could see the door of the closet open just a crack and the evil faces of Balcom and Zita peer out.

He did not move nor did he in any way betray what he saw, but nonchalantly set the tube of precious metal down and pretended to seek something from the table. He turned slowly and retraced his steps to the library below, where he entered, holding his fingers to his lips in warning to Eva not to speak. He walked quickly over to a writing-desk, took a pencil, and began to write.

"Balcom and Zita are listening on the dictagraph. Pretend to quarrel with me."

Eva read in amazement as he wrote. Quickly she comprehended. Then they walked silently until they were almost under the chandelier which held the transmitter of the dictagraph.

"I have something I want to say to you, Mr. Locke," began

Eva, with a wink and a smile at him, "and it grieves me to say it."

"What is it?" asked Locke, with distinct anxiety, winking back.

"I am afraid I shall have to dispense with your services," continued Eva, as she reached out her hand and gave Locke's a little squeeze.

Up-stairs, Balcom and Zita listened intently, their heads close together so that each could catch every word. Balcom was nodding with satisfaction. Each looked at the other as though they could hardly believe their ears.

"But I have tried to serve and protect you," protested Locke, as his face wreathed in smiles at Eva, who was carrying the deception off perfectly. Then he added, plaintively, "I am sorry that I have failed."

"Your protection has led me into danger," returned Eva, in her best voice to denote anger, "and your seeming interest is out of place—and, besides, *Mr.* Locke, Paul Balcom does not like your being here. You know he is the man I am to marry."

As she said this, Eva looked roguishly at him. Locke's face clouded a little, although he knew it was only in a joke.

"But, Miss Brent," he continued to protest, "I had hoped—"

"Not another word, Mr. Locke," interrupted Eva, as she edged very close to him and gazed into his eyes. "Please leave this house at once—I hate you!" And, not suiting the action to the word, she reached out and gave his hand a squeeze that told more than words what her true thoughts in the matter were.

Locke leaned over and was on the point of kissing her when she held up her hand and pointed to the receiver above in the chandelier as if it really had eyes as well as ears. He looked up and was forced to check a laugh lest it be heard by the listeners above.

In the laboratory, Balcom had heard enough. He turned to Zita, and with a hurried command told her to go downstairs.

"Keep an eye on him and tell me where he goes," was the parting instruction of Balcom as the two separated on the stairs at the very time that Paul blustered in the front door.

"Morning, Governor," nodded Paul, as he gave his hat to the butler.

"A very good morning, Paul," emphasized Balcom, quite unctuously, as he went on to tell his son of the supposed quarrel between Eva and Locke which he had overheard.

A light of triumph came into Paul's eyes. Eva's happiness, even her life, meant nothing to him. She was merely a means to his own evil ends and he now felt sure that he held her in his grasp. Besides, in so far as such a selfish nature can care for another human being, Paul cared for De Luxe Dora. There was a fascination for him in her tigerish, unscrupulous nature that a good woman could never inspire.

And now, as he eagerly listened to his father, he visualized new motor-cars, a yacht, rivers of champagne, a life of mad gaiety with his favorite pals, men and women.

Locke, in the library, was laughing quietly with Eva over the success of the ruse. But there was, notwithstanding, an undercurrent of seriousness running through their thoughts. For, although they had scored against their adversaries in misleading them as to their intentions, both realized that Balcom was a tremendously clever man, astute and wise beyond the average in the ways of the world, and that the slightest lack of caution, the smallest flaw in the acting of the parts they had elected to play, would inevitably lose for them the advantage they had gained.

They went into the most minute details of the plans they had formulated, and they realized that in order to keep the wool pulled over Balcom's and Paul's eyes it was necessary that they separate, at least apparently, for a few days. Locke gave out that he was to seek evidence in the lower quarters of the city, while Eva was to play the game at home. It was to Eva that the more difficult role fell.

Locke bade her an affectionate farewell and left by a door opposite to the one leading to the main hallway, where the voices of Paul and his father were now audible.

Eva opened the hallway door and greeted Paul, feigning delight and chiding him for his long absence—which had not been even a day—intimating that there must be some woman in whom he was interested. She made a pretty show of jealousy.

Paul, wearing his vanity on his sleeve, was delighted and his eyes shone with satisfaction. He took a step forward and attempted to take Eva in his arms. But she evaded him playfully, while he pursued her. Finally she could bear no more. The game revolted her. She made the excuse that she must attend her father, and ran up-stairs.

So a day or two passed, days which were sheer torture to Eva. Paul called every day, bringing her little gifts, and it must be acknowledged that he showed exquisite taste.

They took long walks together. On horseback they cantered all over the country. Friends called, and it was at such times that Eva found her only relief from Paul's attentions. Many a rubber of bridge she played just to escape being alone with him.

CHAPTER XVI

At last, late one afternoon, the faithful old butler announced to Eva privately that Locke was on the wire and wished to speak to her.

Eva almost ran to the telephone, and her hand shook with sheer joy as she took the receiver.

"Yes, everything is moving along even more rapidly than I expected," replied Locke to her eager inquiry. "Whenever Paul leaves Brent Rock he goes directly to a miserable cafe and there I see him with a number of people of the underworld. He seems to have a great deal of influence over them. I'm sifting all the clues, and as soon as I unmask him I will send for you."

Eva gave him a brief outline of how she had fared in his absence and an account of her father's condition, which was now very bad. Everything the doctor had done seemed to be without effect.

Locke assured her that he hoped soon to lay hands on the antidote that would restore Brent to health and sanity, and begged Eva to be brave in the mean time.

When the conversation was over Eva felt certain that no one had overheard what she and Quentin had said. But she was

Arthur B. Reeve and John W. Grey

mistaken, as she was to learn at her cost. For, far down in the bowels of the earth, in the den of the Automaton, an emissary had tapped in on the telephone wire and had heard every word.

Down-town, among the haunts of Paul, on the west side, was the Black Tom Cafe. Every attempt had been made to make the place bizarre. About the walls were palings that represented a back fence, along which crawled painted black cats in every conceivable state—a rather odd conceit for a cabaret.

Although the sun had not yet set, the electric lights were already agleam. On a raised platform three weary-eyed musicians were pounding and thumping out the latest Broadway hit.

There were not half a dozen people in the place, and these were obviously denizens of this quarter of the town. They were listless and weary, mere shells of human beings. And yet it was such as these that the slumming parties at night romantically dubbed bohemians.

They showed scant interest as De Luxe Dora, unaccompanied for once, swept into the place. Dora was gorgeously and flashily dressed and fairly scintillated with jewels. She seated herself not far from the door and ordered a cocktail. Then she whistled a bar of music suggestively to the piano-player, who immediately caught it, and the "orchestra" with a show of animation strummed out her suggestion. She sent over drinks for them and was rewarded with more song hits.

Jauntily now Paul came in. A couple of men roused themselves and slouched over to him. They held a whispered conversation, and Paul was insistent on some point. He evidently had his way, for the men slunk back to their places and, sprawling out, were in a moment as listless as before.

Paul nodded to Dora in greeting, but she turned her back. He gave a low whistle of astonishment and went over to her.

"Say, Dora, why the grouch?" he asked.

For a moment she disdained to answer and glared at him witheringly. Then she blurted out, "You're throwing me down for that baby face with the money!"

Paul gave a short laugh and shrugged his shoulders. "Don't be silly," he laughed. "She'll be our meal-ticket."

He sat down, and over a couple more cocktails he had Dora quite mollified.

A few moments later Locke entered and slipped quickly into a chair, since he did not wish to be seen. In his hand he carried a newspaper which he now unfolded and held up in front of him so that it hid his face. Next he poked a hole through the center of the sheet so that he could see without being seen.

At this moment, seemingly in all earnestness, Paul and Dora resumed their quarrel, and Dora's strident voice echoed through the cafe.

"If you throw me down you'd better look out," she bawled.

Paul jumped up, and for a moment it looked as though he would strike her. But he changed his mind, cursed her, and finally stalked out of the cafe.

Locke folded his paper, paid his bill to the sleepy waiter, and started after Paul. At the entrance he stopped, thought a moment, and then went directly to Dora's table and sat down.

"Why, what are you doing here?" she gasped, in great surprise. "Don't you know that you may be *killed?*"

"It's a risk that I must run," replied Locke. "But tell me—you tried to kill me once—why?"

"Because I was a fool, controlled by my love for Paul Balcom—the beast! I hate him!"

Dora drank viciously, then, with jealous venom, leaned over to Locke, and asked, "If that girl, Eva Brent, finds out about him, will she throw him over?"

Locke played the game diplomatically, and apparently succeeded in further incensing Dora against her lover, for, suddenly she jumped up.

"Meet me here in an hour. I'll have everything arranged to spoil Paul Balcom's game," she whispered, as she swept out of the cafe with demi-mondaine majesty.

Locke was elated at the thought of having won so powerful an enemy to his side. But, had he heard Dora's remark to Paul as she met him around a convenient corner, his elation would have given way to caution.

Paul eagerly questioned her with a glance as she approached.

"Well, he fell for it," she announced, toughly, then added, "just as you fell for his dictagraph game with the girl."

There was just a bit of jealousy yet in the tone of Dora. She was not yet convinced of her complete triumph over Eva.

At the same time Locke left the cafe and entered a telephone-booth, from which he called up Eva.

"Come to the Black Tom immediately," he said. "Dora is now on our side and we'll learn the truth, she promises."

Eva at once started to get ready so that she would arrive at the time Locke had fixed, while he loitered in the neighborhood, waiting until the hour agreed upon with Dora was almost gone.

Dora was already waiting for him outside the place when he returned to the Black Tom.

"How is everything?" inquired Locke.

"All arranged. You'll get Paul right."

Just then a man slouched past.

"Follow that fellow," whispered Dora.

Locke nodded and did so.

The man proceeded into the cafe and Locke followed. But instead of sitting down in the main room the man passed through into an inner room. Locke followed. He looked about. It seemed to be a sort of storeroom, as nearly as he could make out.

His guide pressed a secret panel and, stepping through an aperture, beckoned Locke to follow. Locke drew his automatic and went ahead in the inky blackness that lay beyond the panel. The next moment the very floor under his feet seemed to give way. He felt himself thrown down bodily into a sort of subcellar.

Locke was immediately pounced upon by lurking emissaries who seized him after a terrific battle and held him firmly.

"Where's a rope?" growled one.

There was no answer as the men struggled. The question was repeated. Apparently one of them looked about.

"Use the wire," he growled.

The questioner gave a grunt of brutal satisfaction. There in this storeroom lay a huge roll of barbed wire. Coil after coil of this barbed wire was wound about Locke as he struggled, but ever more feebly, for with each coil now the barbs began to cut cruelly into his flesh.

Some one lighted a candle and by its light he saw many carboys of acid standing in a row.

Directly behind them, so that there could be no doubt of the horrible fate in store for him, stood the Automaton.

Already at the entrance to the Black Tom Cafe Eva's speedy runabout came to a stop. Dora was at the curb to meet her and was all winning smiles.

Instinctively Eva shrank from this overdressed woman. But it had been Locke's desire that she come to this place, and she decided to follow the woman, for would it not lead to the unmasking of Paul, whom she hated?

Once or twice on the descent into the cafe Eva hesitated, but was gently urged on by Dora.

Eva was utterly disgusted by the flotsam and jetsam in human guise that she found sprawling at the tables, but she decided to brave the place.

"Wait a moment and I'll get Mr. Locke," smiled Dora.

For a moment, the better to blot out the distasteful scene, Eva closed her eyes.

When she opened them again it was to look into the ferocious, bestial face of the giant emissary who, with fingers clutched like the talons of some foul bird, was reaching toward her to grasp her by the throat.

In the noisome cellar Locke lay as though fascinated by the dread form that confronted him, as well as by its more dreadful purpose.

The Automaton drew back its massive foot and deliberately kicked over one after another of the carboys.

A pungent odor at once permeated the cellar air as the acid ate into the floor.

Its purpose accomplished, the Automaton stalked toward Locke, and stood towering above him.

Would it crush out Locke's life under its ponderous heel? Or would it leave him to a death more horrible?

Like writhing serpents, the rivulets of seething, burning acid crept closer, closer.

CHAPTER XVII

The Automaton and its emissaries left the cellar. In the distance a door slammed and Locke was left to his terrible fate.

Except for the gurgling of the flowing acid and the scampering of the rats all was silent.

Locke tried to move. But the sharp barbs of the wire cut into his flesh, a torture to test the fortitude of a stoic.

Moreover, Locke had barely recovered from the shock of his fall into the cellar. Thus for a few seconds that seemed to him to be ages he lay there watching the fiery death creep closer. Then the will to live surged through him and he struggled furiously to escape from the deadly path of the acid. Gone now was his flinching and shrinking as the sharp barbs lacerated his tender flesh. Gone was the calmness that denoted surrender and the acceptance of his fate.

With bunching muscles he writhed inch by inch to one side, out of the path of the flow of the acid. He was just in time, for, at his last mighty effort, the consuming fluid flowed past, not an inch from his face.

To extricate himself from the coils of the wire was a slow and painful task. Wounded with a hundred wounds, with each movement of his body adding a further injury, many times Locke was forced to desist in his efforts to free himself. However, he persisted, though, strong man that he was, the tears of agony burned his eyes and beads of cold sweat stood on his brow even before the first coil was loosened.

He could not, even to save his own life, have persisted in this self-inflicted torture had it not been for the thought of Eva hurrying to this dreadful den. That thought almost drove him mad and spurred him to furious effort.

It was well that it did. For at this very moment the beastly emissary in the cafe above was closing in on her.

Locke gave a final heave and tugged at the last strands of the wire that held him prisoner. His clothes ripped to tatters and his flesh torn and lacerated, he at last stood free.

Without an instant's pause he collected packing-cases and even barrels. He stacked them one upon the other, pyramiding them under the trap-door through which he had fallen into the cellar. Then he climbed upon them, leaped, and tried to grasp the edge of the floor above him, but fell short and came tumbling down amid the boxes and barrels, only to start stacking them up all over again.

Finally he managed to grasp the edge of the floor with one hand and draw himself up. For a few moments he lay panting on the floor, then groped for the panel through which he had entered not half an hour before. It was locked, but a shrewd kick above the lock opened it to him and he rushed through the storeroom and out into the now brilliantly lighted cafe.

He was barely in time.

Arthur B. Reeve and John W. Grey

The emissary already had Eva in his grasp and was choking her into unconsciousness. The foul habitues of the resort, far from aiding the poor girl, seemed for the first time that day to be showing interest and to be thoroughly enjoying the brutal sight.

With a shout Locke charged. His right swing landed just behind the emissary's ear and the man dropped, pulling Eva down with him. But Locke had her up and behind him in a second.

Three other emissaries appeared as though by magic and attacked him on all sides.

Locke's automatic had been lost when he fell into the cellar. Consequently he grabbed up one of the cafe chairs, which he wielded like a club.

One emissary had worked around until he was at one side of Locke and almost behind him, a blackjack raised in his hand. But Eva warned Locke in time. Whirling about, he made a full swing with the chair and caught the emissary full in the face with it. The man went down and stayed down.

"Run quick as you can," panted Locke to Eva. "Get the car started."

She was reluctant to leave him, and Locke saw that delay was dangerous. He hurled what remained of the chair into the faces of the last two emissaries, then turned and rushed up the steps, carrying Eva along with him.

A whir of the starter, the throbbing of the engine as the gas in the cylinders ignited, and they were streaking toward Brent Rock, safe.

In a still fashionable, but older, part of the town, the elder Balcom had his quarters. They were spacious and furnished in Oriental style, with many a suggestion of the Indian Ocean.

Balcom was evidently annoyed, and seriously so. He was striding up and down the apartment, scowling and puffing furiously at a black cigar. In his hand was a letter, and from time to time he halted and glanced at it, then fell back to his quick walking again, while a sinister light came into his eyes. Yet the contents of the note were hardly such as would have seemed likely to cause a man of honest purpose any agitation.

MR. HERBERT BALCOM,

International Patents, Inc.

DEAR SIR,—A special meeting of the executive board of International Patents, Inc., will be called at Brent Rock this afternoon to determine the future policies of this company.

[Signed] EVA BRENT.

Balcom had read the notice for the tenth time when a negro servant entered and announced that his son Paul wished to see him.

"Show him in—then," growled Balcom to the servant.

Paul entered. He was evidently somewhat chagrined and crestfallen. Nor did his father's next words tend to cheer him up.

"I suppose you'll acknowledge that you've made a miserable mess of it," accused the older man. "When will you stop mixing women with business?"

Paul was silent. Indeed there was nothing that he could say.

"And now look at this note," pursued Balcom, in growing rage. "It brings things to a head. What can we do?"

He thrust the note at Paul, who read it. Balcom himself reread it, crumpled it in anger, tore it, and threw the pieces in violence on the floor.

This time it was to be Paul who was to formulate a plan. It was of such a dark and criminal nature that even Herbert Balcom, hardened as he was himself, was for the moment appalled at his son's temerity. But as he listened to Paul's words they fascinated him and he leaned forward the better to take in the scheme.

As Paul and his father planned, it seemed that here was power unlimited, wealth beyond all counting and without the possibility of discovery. For, like most men of his caliber, the approbation of the community was dear to Balcom.

"Good, Paul!" approved Balcom. "Go to it at once."

Paul looked keenly at his father.

"Haven't you anything to add?"

"No, I have nothing to advise. The scheme is perfect, and as you conceived it you can also execute it. The best of luck to you, my boy."

A few moments later Paul went out, his dark face beaming at being reinstated in his father's good graces. He was full of his plan.

Down in one of the city's worst sections and near the river-front there stood an old ramshackle building. Why it had not been condemned by the building inspectors was a mystery. But it stood in all its squalid ugliness. The door and the windows were locked and shuttered. One could see at a glance that the building had been long unused.

There was an alley strewn with tin cans and other refuse leading to the back of the house, and it was down a flight of broken brick steps that Old Meg, the fortune-teller, had her den where through the superstitions of those inhabiting the neighborhood she managed to eke out a miserable existence. The interior of the den was unspeakably filthy. The furniture consisted of a broken-down couch, a chest of drawers in a like condition, a card-table, a few kitchen chairs, and some boxes. Most of the panes in the windows had been broken and the empty spaces had been covered with old newspapers. Consequently, a candle thrust into an old wine-bottle supplied the only real light.

At the table, idly shuffling a pack of grimy cards, sat Old Meg, a horrible old hag, wrinkled in face like a mummy, with only the stumps of teeth which had more the appearance of tusks. Her unkempt hair was matted and ugly wisps of it hung down over her bleary eyes. For clothes she wore an old-fashioned faded gingham wrapper and around her shoulders a dirty torn shawl. On her feet was a pair of man's shoes, many sizes too large, which had evidently been cast away as useless by some former owner, himself squalid. These she managed to keep on by tying the tops with wrapping-cord. A more unlovely human being it would have been hard to find in all the great city. There she sat, crooning a ballad to herself in a high, cracked voice. It sounded like an incantation.

A step sounded in the alley and Old Meg looked up and listened intently. The sound came nearer. She got up and retreated into a dark corner, for she knew the neighborhood well, and many a time some thug, brutal with drink, had entered her den and wrung her last few pennies from her.

But it was no inhabitant of this quarter of the town who entered this time. It was Paul Balcom.

The hag grinned in a horrible way at him, for it was not unusual for people of his kind to visit her and it always meant money. With her apron she dusted off the chair that stood at the table and begged him to be seated. Then she shuffled the cards and cut, shuffled and cut, and then as though at last satisfied she laid them face downward on the table and spoke.

"Wish, my handsome gentleman, and may your wish come true."

"Go ahead with the hocus-pocus," growled Paul.

Mother Meg picked up one card after another and her cracked voice was evidently following a set formula.

"If the queen of spades comes between the king of clubs and the queen of hearts—"

Paul listened with a strained intentness as the hag singsonged on and on. Then a look of satisfaction came into his eyes and he smiled happily. Next his look changed to a nasty look of determination, and he abruptly got up, tossing a bank-note on the table which Old Meg grabbed with avidity, calling down Heaven's blessings on the handsome gentleman until Paul, running up-stairs, could hear no more.

Paul returned immediately to his father's apartment, where Balcom was impatiently waiting for him. He described minutely Old Meg, her eagerness for money, and the squalid quarters in which she lived. The elder Balcom seemed satisfied and they left the apartment together.

"Paul," directed Balcom, "get out to Brent Rock as soon as you can while I make arrangements with this Old Meg."

Balcom stepped into his own car, while Paul hailed a taxicab, and a few minutes later Balcom alighted before the house of Old Meg. He walked down the alley and descended into the den.

As before, Meg was in hiding in a dark corner until she could ascertain just who her visitor might be. Seeing Balcom, she came out and courtesied and scraped as she had for Paul.

Balcom announced the object of his visit immediately, and while he was speaking he fingered a roll of bills which he had taken from his pocket the better to arouse the old hag's avariciousness.

It had the desired effect and her eyes fairly gleamed with the craving of possession.

"Do as I tell you, Meg," directed Balcom, "and I'll make you rich. Do you understand? Rich!" he emphasized, rolling out the last word silkily on his tongue.

Old Meg's last scruples, had she ever had even one, fell before this temptation and she became almost the slave of Balcom.

Balcom now gave a command and the old hag sidled to the door of an inner room.

"Jimmy! Jimmy!" she called. "Come here to me."

In a moment a boy slunk into the room. He was sharp-faced, pinched for food, and in tatters, as disreputable-looking as the hag herself. Meg whispered something to him, and, as though galvanized by an electric current, the boy shot up-stairs. He was soon back again with two brutal-looking men who looked suspiciously at Balcom and then shuffled into a corner, where they conferred eagerly with Old Meg.

At first it was plain to be seen that they were refusing to do her bidding, but Meg made a movement as though she were counting money. After that it was equally plain that they agreed.

Meg sidled over to Balcom and he unwrapped a few bills of large denomination and handed them to her. She immediately hid them in her dress, with many a furtive look toward her accomplices.

Balcom's eyes followed those of the old hag, and, realizing that his whole conspiracy might fail unless the men were assured of further reward on the completion of their task, he approached them smoothly.

"Of course," he insinuated, "you understand that if you three follow instructions to the letter I'll double that amount." Then he left the place, brushing his coat with his handkerchief as he did so. "Brent Rock," he said to his chauffeur, curtly, as he stepped into his car.

CHAPTER XVIII

Eva and Locke were seated at a long table in the library of Eva's home. Before them were many ledgers of International Patents, Incorporated. Eva was reading certain entries in the books, while Locke was making notes to be used at the coming directors' meeting.

Eva closed the ledger from which she had been reading and announced, "I intend, at the meeting, to insist that the patents held in the Graveyard of Genius be released to the world."

"It is the only honorable thing to do," agreed Locke. "You will undoubtedly meet with violent opposition from Balcom and some few who owe their fortunes to him, but in the end you will win."

"If we could only have found the antidote," sighed Eva, "and my father could only be again in control of things."

"All we can do is to act as we think he would have acted if he were in control," soothed Locke.

"May I speak to you a moment, Mr. Locke?" interrupted a voice.

It was Zita who had entered noiselessly and now stood well

Arthur B. Reeve and John W. Grey

within the room.

How long had she been there? How much had she overheard? Both Eva and Quentin exchanged worried glances.

Locke rose and went over to Zita, who spoke to him in a whispered undertone.

The matter was so trivial that it hardly warranted her intrusion. Locke was puzzled. But he was a man and, therefore, did not understand. For, as Zita continued, there was a world of longing in her eyes. She even went so far as to finger the lapel of his coat.

Eva understood only too well, and her face crimsoned. She bit her lips, and in vexation at Zita her finger-nails pressed into her palms. Paul's entrance at this moment was a distinct relief, much as she despised the man.

"What's all the fuss about?" he inquired.

Paul had a gaiety of manner that he could slip on like a coat, and it was this quality that made him dangerous. He was popular and attractive.

Paul took Eva's hand and managed to hold it just the fraction of a second longer than was necessary to convey friendship. Then Eva withdrew her hand, but not before Locke saw it and scowled.

It was not long before the elder Balcom also arrived.

"Good afternoon, my children," he greeted, jovially. "I'm just a bit ahead of time, I imagine. But why you children don't leave dry matters of business to us older heads I'm blessed if I know."

"Mr. Balcom," retorted Eva, keenly, "the older head that would protect my interests and the interests of those poor inventors lies stricken, as you know, in the room above. In his absence the children, as you are pleased to call us, will do their best."

Balcom glared, while Zita with a strange glance toward Eva left Locke and joined Balcom in a far corner of the room.

"Zita," Balcom whispered, "the time has arrived to take you out of this false position."

Zita trembled with suppressed excitement as she heard this, and followed Balcom back toward the table, where the others were already seating themselves.

It was approaching the hour, when Eva rose and was about to speak. Balcom motioned and stopped her with a gesture.

"One moment, please, Miss Brent," he interrupted. "Before the others arrive I am going to establish Zita's real position in this house."

All at the table looked at one another in openly expressed astonishment. Zita, with eyes cast down, hands clasped in her lap, seemed almost demure, though about her mouth played a faint smile.

Even Paul did not understand this phase of the conspiracy and looked at his father as much as to say, "I wonder what the old man is up to now?"

Locke was the first to recover his coolness. "Just what, Mr. Balcom, do you mean?" he asked.

"I mean—" began Balcom, then stopped. "But first I will produce a witness who can vouch for all the facts which I am about to relate."

Balcom went to the door and opened it. There, bobbing her head and smirking mechanically, stood that loathsome creature, Old Meg. In these rich surroundings her frightful squalor was all the more accentuated. Those at the table drew back in utter disgust as she tottered into the room. As she passed Zita she paused.

"I held you in these arms when you were but a wee baby," she muttered, hideously.

Zita drew away from her and looked at Balcom questioningly. Balcom now leaned far over the table and spoke impressively.

"Twenty years ago Brent was secretly married to his secretary. There was a child. But Brent craved money, and power that the money would bring. Saddled with a wife and child, he was barred from his ambition, which was to marry some rich woman. So he made a hell on earth for his wife until, in desperation, she consented to an annulment of their marriage."

The room was breathlessly quiet as Balcom continued.

"Years passed and then his conscience smote him. He made his own child his secretary." Then he turned to Zita, pointing at her. "There she sits," he exclaimed, "and half of the voting power of this company belongs to her—Zita Brent, Zita Dane *Brent*."

Instantly Locke was on his feet.

"Balcom, you lie!" he rasped.

"Lie or no lie," retorted Balcom, "as vice-president of the

company I refuse to permit any action to be taken until Zita's position is legally established."

Locke turned to Eva. "Miss Brent," he asked, with a bow, "may I speak for you?"

Eva nodded.

"Then, Balcom," remarked Locke, "we shall carry the proposed motion over your head. You cannot produce sufficient proofs to retard our action."

"My protests," sneered Balcom, as he strode toward the door, "will be entered in the minutes of this meeting."

Zita, in the excitement, had already disappeared. Paul bowed to Eva and Locke mockingly and followed his father.

Old Meg squeezed herself against the walls of the library and was trying to get out of the room without being detected. But Locke was too alert for her and caught her by the shoulder, detaining her. She tried to fight him off with her feeble arms. Again and again he tried to question her.

"The story is true, I tell you, gospel true," Meg repeated over and over again.

Locke let her go and she started toward the door. Then the habit of a lifetime overcame her and she turned.

"If you would know the truth, my pretty," she croaked at Eva, "come to Old Meg." Then she hobbled out.

Eva was naturally perturbed, although Locke tried to comfort her. Yet she could not forget what had happened between him and Zita just before the meeting, and, woman-like, she now held aloof.

"Eva," pleaded Locke, "won't you trust me? Things are in such a critical state that we must not have any misunderstanding."

But Eva merely tossed her pretty head. "I don't care for Zita or her actions," she replied, petulantly.

Locke diplomatically changed the subject. "I believe," he said, slowly, "that that old hag is in the pay of either Paul or his father, and I mean to find out which it is."

Locke had started across the hallway when Eva called him back.

"Quentin," she said, earnestly, "I trust you—absolutely." Then she hid her face in her hands and almost ran into the dining-room.

Had she been a moment sooner she would have caught that mysterious person, Doctor Q, who had entered the house some time before, and, on overhearing heated words coming from the library, had remained with his ear glued to the keyhole, absorbing every word that was said until Balcom left. But he had shuffled away before she ran in.

Back in Old Meg's den some time later the little gutter rat who, a few hours before, had brought the two thugs back to Balcom and Old Meg was coiled up in a corner, asleep.

With light footsteps that did not awaken the sleeping boy, a strange little figure now came scurrying down the brick stairs. The figure hesitated a moment, then entered the foul den.

In tatters, like the sleeping street gamin, this other boy still had something winsome, something elusively handsome, about him, a certain refinement of features. However, a black patch over one eye showed that this gamin was manly enough, evidently, when it came to fighting. He stirred the sleeping boy with his foot, and the boy, cursing volubly and beyond his years, roused himself.

They talked excitedly in whispers and the boy who had just entered gave the street arab some money. Then together they tiptoed into the other room and down a flight of rickety steps into the cellar. This cellar connected with another cellar of large size that was used as a storehouse.

The boys barely spoke and, when it was necessary, only in whispers. They came to a pile of cotton bales, found a convenient space between the bales, crawled in, and lay still.

Night was coming fast as the hag, trailed by Locke, left Brent Rock. She walked fast for so old a woman, but, finally, coming to a street-car line, she took the first car that came along. Locke had had the foresight to have himself followed by one of the numerous Brent cars and so was able to keep the street-car in sight until the old woman alighted in her squalid quarter of town. Locke got out of his machine and followed her on foot, keeping close to the walls of the buildings to avoid having her see him.

Old Meg turned the corner that ran alongside her dwelling, and there, for the first time, gave an indication that she was aware that she was being followed. She chuckled to herself, gave a few stumbling capers which might have been an imitation of a dance step, then waved her hand. Was it a signal?

Locke was never to reach the alley. Old Meg had whipped around the corner so quickly that for a moment he was puzzled as to just where she had disappeared. He stopped with his back half turned to a flight of stairs leading down to the cellar entrance of a big warehouse. Suddenly he was sent stumbling forward to his knees, half dazed by a treacherous blow dealt from behind.

He was up again in an instant and was defending himself from the attack of half a dozen thugs. He put up a splendid fight, but the odds were too great, and in a few minutes he was down on the ground, unconscious and bound.

The emissaries of the Automaton, for such they were, carried him down the steps and into the warehouse cellar.

Already, on leaving Brent Rock, Paul Balcom had not been idle. He had been immediately driven to a telegraph-office, where, after having used nearly an entire pad of blanks, he succeeded in composing the following message:

DEAREST QUENTIN,—Have proofs that Old Meg spoke the truth. Meet me immediately at her place.

ZITA.

The message was addressed to Locke at Brent Rock and was marked "Important."

"That ought to fetch her!" muttered Paul, as he left the office.

Twenty minutes or so later the telegram was delivered to the butler at Brent Rock, who brought it at once to Eva.

At first she was loath to open a message addressed to some one else. But Quentin's affairs and her own were so inter-twined by this time that she felt that the telegram would, in all probability, concern her as well as Locke. She tore it open.

"Dearest Quentin," she read and for a minute could get no farther, for it seemed as if a mist had formed before her eyes.

She clutched at the balustrade. Then pride, jealousy, and a certain anger surged up within her and she finished reading the telegram.

Eva was in a quandary what to do. She paced up and down the hallway, biting her lips and repressing the tears.

Could it be possible, after all, that Locke was faithless? Was this the man who had been so kind, who had saved her from a thousand dangers? At any rate, she would find out once and for all.

Faint and heart-sick, she gave orders to have her runabout brought around. It was a long drive from Brent Rock, but Eva's fast speedster covered the ground quickly. Twice policemen tried to stop her and, failing, probably took the number of her car. Nothing could deter her. And, as the cool evening wind lashed her face, faith in Locke revived and the suspicion came that she might be rushing into danger. But no thought of herself entered her mind as she stepped on the accelerator and the car shot forward. Her single thought was of speed, more speed, to get to Locke quickly.

She was appalled at the squalor of the neighborhood in which she finally found herself. Disgusted and revolted at the filth of Old Meg's abode, still not for an instant did she falter or hesitate. She ran down the steps to Old Meg's home.

The old hag was evidently awaiting her, for this time she did not hide at the sound of approaching footsteps, but came forward, courtesying and mumbling greetings, while her eyes gleamed with a satisfaction that was positively hellish.

"Mr. Locke—where is he?" Eva gasped.

Arthur B. Reeve and John W. Grey

"All in good time, my pretty, all in good time," mumbled the hag. "You're to wait for him here."

But Eva insisted on seeing Locke at once and the old hag lied volubly. He had been here, and had stepped out for a moment. No, she did not know where—to get a cigar, maybe. Would the pretty lady hear her fortune told while she waited?

As there was apparently nothing that she could do until Locke returned, Eva sat at the card-table while Old Meg droned her old fortune-telling rigamarole.

In spite of her growing fear and agitation Eva became interested. There was something calming in the monotonous voice of the old crone.

"When the queen of spades comes between the jack of hearts and the king of diamonds and the—a—the—"

A door directly behind Eva silently and slowly opened. Stealthily a boy's head was thrust out. On the young face was a world of deadly hatred. As the sputtering candle burned brighter for a moment, startlingly, a vague change was noticeable in the lineaments of the features.

It was the same gamin who had given the sleeping boy money. But now, in the candle-light, with only the head showing, it was no boy who glared malevolently at Eva, but a woman—and that woman was the implacable Zita!

The head disappeared to give place to the visages of two horrible-looking men, the same brutes who were present when Balcom had spread the net of his conspiracy.

"When the jack of clubs," droned the witch, "and the—"

With barely a sound the two thugs entered the room behind Eva. In the hand of one was an old gunny sack.

"—and the queen of hearts—"

Eva was so interested now that she leaned far over the table, her eyes fastened on the cards as they fell.

A thug stumbled. Eva, startled, sat back quickly and tried to rise. But the next instant she felt herself struggling in the heavy folds of the grimy gunny sack.

The emissaries, carrying Locke, had staggered with their burden into the warehouse cellar until, coming to a closed door, one of them rapped on it in a peculiar manner that was evidently a signal. An instant, and the door opened.

Through it stalked the Automaton.

The monster gazed intently at Locke as though to determine whether it were indeed he, then waved the emissaries on to the shaft of a huge freight elevator.

In the shaft, directly under the elevator platform, they now cast Locke's unconscious body.

"Are you sure the watchman's still up above?" asked one.

"Sure."

"Then give a ring for the basement."

A thug pressed the button that signaled. In a moment, creaking and groaning, the massive elevator started to descend.

A shuffling of feet was heard and down the stairs leading

from Old Meg's quarters came the two thugs carrying Eva. A few feet behind them, still in boy's clothes, was Zita.

The jar to his body as the emissaries threw him on the concrete floor had tended to bring Locke back to consciousness. For a moment he lay still. Then the sound of the descending elevator attracted his attention. He gazed upward and dimly saw the slowly moving platform. In a flash he realized his danger.

Locke struggled fiercely to dislodge his bonds. He contorted his body, expanded his powerful chest in an effort to break the ropes that held him a prisoner.

At this moment the thugs that were carrying Eva passed by, followed by others. Apparently they took no notice of him, but continued on their way with the helpless girl.

Locke, his own danger forgotten, became frantic with apprehension for her and tore savagely at the restraining ropes.

Zita stopped. Her face was a study of conflicting emotions as she saw Locke struggling at the bottom of the shaft.

Floor by floor, inch by inch, the enormous elevator, that would crush out Locke's life as though he were an insect, continued to descend.

Zita stepped to an electric switch. That switch would stop the elevator immediately and save Locke's life.

She raised her hand—and then, looking after the retreating thugs and emissaries, she saw Eva again. Zita's lips formed a cruel line and a flinty hardness came into her eyes.

Her hand dropped.

There were only a few feet between Locke and the descending elevator. Locke was struggling frenziedly to escape and rescue Eva.

Zita's hand went out again and grasped the handle of the switch.

She hesitated, hate on her face.

Would she, for love of Locke, who had not returned her love, save him?

Could she bring herself to save this man—for a woman she hated, who had won him from her?

If she saved him it would be only to lose him to the other woman.

With a great creaking the massive elevator was within only a few short inches of Locke.

CHAPTER XIX

Every fiber of Zita's body was galvanized into action as she threw the whole weight of her body against the elevator emergency-control switch.

There was a sputtering of blue flame as the connection was made, and Zita closed her eyes. With a shudder she heard the great elevator strike the cellar floor and then rebound.

She dared not open her eyes. The last thing that she had seen was Locke struggling frantically to escape from under the elevator that was only a few inches above him and seemed destined to crush out his life.

Slowly, fearfully, she opened her eyes. Locke's body lay motionless at her feet, separated almost literally by only the breadth of a hair from the shaft.

The relief, the reaction from her terrible emotions, made Zita half hysterical. Trembling in every limb, she made her way to Locke and fell on her knees by him. She wrapped her arms about him and held his head up.

It was thus that she was holding him when his eyes slowly opened and gazed questioningly into her own, his brow knitted in perplexity.

Then, with a rush, it all came back to him—the descending elevator, Zita standing at the switch, while his life hung in the balance, his last frantic effort to escape just before the descending elevator had grazed his head, rendering him unconscious. That Zita, at the last moment, had attempted to save his life he did not know, nor why she now gazed at him frankly with eyes of love.

It was all inexplicable to him.

Another instant and he had wrenched himself loose from Zita's arms and was struggling with the ropes that still bound him even after he had managed to roll out from under the elevator in the last nick of time.

He had suddenly realized that the sight of Eva being carried off by the emissaries had not been a hideous dream, but a terrible actuality, and that at this very moment she was probably in the most imminent danger.

Zita realized that he wanted freedom to rush to Eva's assistance. Had she dared, she would have refused to release him from her arms, would at least have hindered his untying his bonds. But there was a masterful something about his silent demand to be released that would admit of no refusal.

In a few seconds Locke completed the freeing of himself and was dashing madly toward the door through which the gang, carrying Eva, had passed.

The door was unlocked, and, hesitating not an instant, Quentin dashed through and into a large room.

Eva, the gunny sack removed and still unconscious, lay on the floor. The emissaries were grouped around her. In the background, dimly visible, stood the iron monster.

Arthur B. Reeve and John W. Grey

Startled, they looked up as Locke rushed into the room. But before they could do more, Locke had whipped out his automatic and, point-blank, was blazing away at the murderous crew. Two emissaries fell dead or mortally wounded. The others scattered.

Only the Automaton, man of iron that he was, showed no sign of fear. Instead, he advanced ponderously upon Locke.

The automatic barked again, but did not succeed in deterring the monster. Locke realized the futility of using this puny weapon against such a foe.

He dashed toward Eva. It was the work of only an instant to snatch her up, practically from under the monster's feet, to turn, and to carry her through the door by which he had been brought in. Holding her in one arm, he slammed the door shut and shot the bolt.

He was just in time, for the next instant the door bulged out beneath the dead weight of the Automaton as it hurled its massive form against the other side.

Zita vas still waiting at the elevator shaft when Locke, carrying Eva in his arms, entered. At the sight Zita's whole body expressed her unquenched hatred of the unconscious girl. Her eyes narrowed, her lips became livid, and her hands clenched as though she would like to strike the helpless Eva.

"Zita," demanded Locke, suspiciously, "why did you hesitate to save my life?"

"Because," she replied—and her voice indicated the force of her answer whether it were really the truth or not—"I love you, and would not save you—for *her*."

Zita turned and ran up the stairs leading to Old Meg's as

Locke turned to try to revive Eva.

But the hammer blows of the monster resounded through-out the cellar. At any moment the door might come crashing down and Locke and Eva might again be at the mercy of the iron fiend.

Locke caught up Eva in his arms again and, groping, sought the exit of the warehouse.

He dared not follow Zita through Old Meg's den. Love that could for any reason hesitate or injure the one loved was incomprehensible to him. He felt that the hag's den might now be but an ambush and that Zita might have run ahead to warn the uninjured emissaries of his coming.

By a lucky chance he found the path leading directly to the warehouse steps and the street. Eva's speedster had not been moved or tampered with and he placed Eva gently in the seat, climbed in, and started the motor. As he did so three emissaries came running out of the alley leading to Old Meg's. But shooting the gears into high speed, Locke easily evaded them and turned up the first corner.

He was going to take Eva to the first doctor's or a drug-store, but it proved not to be necessary. The rush of the air as the car moved rapidly revived her, and in a few moments she was quite herself again, eagerly questioning him about her rescue.

Although they were thankful for their escape, still they could not blind themselves to the fact that all their efforts had been in vain, that they stood no nearer to their great desire, and that, at least until now, their enemies had proved too wily and too strong for them.

But they were young, courageous, and resourceful, and as

they drew up before Brent Rock they were busily engaged with plans for the future.

It was the following afternoon in the Chinese quarter. The Celestials were celebrating one of their numerous feasts. Long multicolored banners and streamers were hanging from every window and balcony and were even strung across the narrow street, almost brushing the faces of the motley throng that passed beneath. Tom-toms and cymbals beat and clashed, while from the Chinese theater came the shrill piping of reeds and the high-pitched chanting voices of Chinamen.

Street venders cried their wares and the windows of the Oriental shops were gaily bedecked for the holiday.

Through the dense happy throng a man made his way. He, too, was an Oriental, but of a different race. A giant in size, he calmly pushed and shoved the smaller Celestials out of his path, and, although they chattered angrily at him, their resentment went no farther, for his size and the menace of his swarthy face made them pause.

Before the entrance of a curio-shop he halted and consulted a card. Then, satisfied that he had found his destination, he picked up a wicker carrying-case that for the moment he had placed on the curb and entered the shop.

A Chinaman stepped forward, scrutinized him closely, and, nodding significantly, bade the new-comer follow him.

They went to the back of the shop. The Chinese clapped his hands, and a panel in the wall slid back, disclosing a stairway. The new-comer stepped through the aperture and the panel closed behind him. He mounted the stairs and came to a room, magnificent in its Oriental splendor.

Priceless rugs covered the floor and walls, while on wonderfully carved teakwood stands reposed ancient porcelains, specimens of bygone dynasties, antique arms and armor cunningly wrought, jades and ivories marvelously fashioned by master craftsmen long since dead. Seen through the filmy haze of rising incense, the room was a veritable treasure-house of Oriental art.

On low settees a few richly clad Chinese were reclining, and in a far corner, gazing intently into a globe of crystal, sat a man of the same race as the new-comer, a Madagascan.

Startled at the entrance of the giant, he left off his shadow-gazing and came hastily forward, cringing as he did so.

The giant, in an impressive, booming voice, now spoke for the first time.

"I, the Strangler, have come from Madagascar with the Great Torture."

A door opened and Doctor Q entered the room, his head wagging from side to side.

As he caught sight of the Madagascan he stopped short and put his hand to his head with a gesture of perplexity, striving piteously to place the stranger. He could not succeed. With a half-running, half-stumbling gait he withdrew to a corner of the room and furtively watched the two Madagascans.

There came the sound of a gong. A panel slid back, and into the room there majestically swept a Chinaman of pure Mongolian type.

He was gorgeously clad in flowing silks and wore the princely cap with a button. At a glance his piercing eye took in every detail of the room. Then he went directly to the Madagascan, whose overbearing air of assurance immediately forsook him at the Chinaman's approach.

He bowed low and reverently, for it was Long Fang to whom he made obeisance, Long Fang, leader of a great Tong, and implacable foe to all others, a Chinese whose tentacles of power reached into every corner of the underworld, spreading terror.

In an incisive, icy voice that sent a chill through the big man's frame, he now spoke.

"You have been overlong on your journey and we have been waiting for you." Then with a menace in his voice he snarled, "It is well for you that you came at last."

The big man shuddered and remained silent. Long Fang crossed to Doctor Q.

"The instrument of torture is here," he said. "The Madagascan has just brought it. He is an unrivaled strangler."

"Let him approach," commanded Doctor Q.

Long Fang beckoned, and the Strangler came forward. His eyes had been fixed on the Chinese, but now they roved to the figure of Doctor Q, and he fell back in consternation, clutching the other Madagascan by the shoulder and gasping in awestruck tones.

"In our country his magic is supreme!"

With difficulty he controlled himself and bowed low, his forehead almost touching the floor. Then he looked away, cringing.

"I see that you recognize me," Doctor Q chuckled, fiendishly. "Good! You will not be so foolish as to fail me."

"No, no, master, I swear it by—"

"Never mind your oath. My power is my guaranty. Go— follow Long Fang. He will direct you to the torture-chamber."

Doctor Q turned on his heel and hobbled out of the room.

Long Fang and the Strangler were about to proceed to the torture-chamber when footsteps were heard on the stairway that led to the curio-shop below. Long Fang and the Madagascan stopped and listened.

Another moment and De Luxe Dora and Paul Balcom stepped into the room. With a curt command Paul called Long Fang to him and the Chinaman, important as he was, hastened to obey.

What was this strange power that Paul, at will, could exercise throughout the underworld?

With a few terse questions Paul ascertained the exact condition of affairs.

"You say, Long Fang, that all is ready?"

"All, master. We only awaited your coming."

Then with a graceful gesture he asked, "Will you so far honor your humble servant?" as he indicated the way into another room.

Dora, followed by Paul and the Chinese, stepped through

the portal and came to a Chinese temple.

It was a large room and the decorations, although equally well executed as those in the room they had just left, were actually terrifying. Flying dragons and serpents done in bronze hung from the ceiling, while on a raised dais at the farther end of the room was an enormous squatting figure of the seven-handed god. Before it, in braziers, fire gleamed, giving off a heavy, pungent odor that was almost over-powering to Occidental nostrils.

On either side of the huge image hung silken curtains, in all probability covering doorways into yet other chambers.

For the first time Dora showed signs of interest. With the shop and the first chamber she was already familiar, but this was something new, something to give the spur to her satiated, *blase* nature. She moved about the place, fingering the rare tapestries, contemplating probably what gorgeous hangings they would make for her own apartment.

Dora's preoccupation gave Long Fang his opportunity to confer with Paul alone and he moved closer to him.

"Master," he nodded, "why not use the beautiful lady to lure the other one into our power?"

Paul shook his head negatively. He knew that Eva was aware that Dora was her enemy.

"But, master," persisted the Chinese, "you told me that this Miss Brent loves her father, and that she would do anything for his recovery. Let this lady tell her that the Madagascan has brought an antidote that will restore his reason. She will come here and we shall trap her."

For a moment Paul stood in deep thought, then called to Dora.

At first she laughed at the idea that Eva would even listen to her. But Dora was clever and conceited and in the end she agreed that at least she would make the attempt.

At this moment in another quarter of town Paul's father was ready to leave his apartment, yet from his nervousness it could readily be seen that he was waiting for some one. A Madagascan servant entered and salaamed.

"Master," he announced, "the Strangler has arrived from Madagascar."

Balcom's face lighted up with intense satisfaction and cunning at the news. He waved the servant away, picked up his hat and stick, and hurried out.

In the library at Brent Rock Eva and Locke were having an earnest conversation. Locke had on his motoring togs and was on the point of going out.

"By elimination," he was saying, "I will prove that either Paul or his father is the Automaton. I am going to trap Paul."

"Quentin," cautioned Eva, "for my sake be careful."

Locke strove to quiet her fears, pointing out that his scheme was necessary in order to save her father, and in the end Eva reluctantly consented.

She went with him to the porte-cochere where his car was already waiting.

"Good luck!" she tried to call cheerfully, in spite of

her misgivings.

Long after his car had disappeared in the distance she stood there gazing after it, a world of anxiety in her eyes.

CHAPTER XX

Darkness had settled down upon Brent Rock, following the departure of Locke, when a trim runabout drew up under the porte-cochere and Dora stepped lightly out of it.

She paused for a moment and looked about curiously. For some time she hesitated. In this house lived the girl whom in her heart Dora hated bitterly.

What sort of reception might she expect? Yet Paul and his underworldlings had played on Dora's pride until they had prevailed on her to undertake the mission. As she looked about all her old assurance came back to her and Dora turned and approached the door boldly.

Eva was just about to go up-stairs to her room when she heard the butler at the door and a woman's voice asking whether Miss Brent was at home. Eva paused a moment.

There was evidently a slight altercation between the butler and the new-comer as the latter raised her voice sharply.

"You will tell Miss Brent I must see her," reiterated Dora.

There was a pause, during which the butler was heard to murmur something, and then the woman's voice was heard again.

Arthur B. Reeve and John W. Grey

"Tell Miss Brent that if she refuses to see me she will regret it all her life."

Eva was intensely interested now, for she recognized the voice of De Luxe Dora. But with her interest there came a feeling of repulsion with which this woman always inspired her, and her first impulse was to have Dora shown out of the house.

The very nature of the danger with which they were all surrounded, however, prohibited such a drastic course. Yet how dare that woman enter Brent Rock?

Still, the very fact of her so daring pointed to some serious matter which Eva felt she ought to know. At any rate, there could be no harm to listen to Dora's reason for coming, and there would probably be much to be learned.

Eva called to the butler and he stepped aside, and Dora, all smiles now, and with her hand extended in greeting, advanced toward Eva, who ignored her extended hand.

"Need I tell you," remarked Eva, coldly, "that I am astounded at your presumption in coming here?"

"Miss Brent," replied Dora, "believe me, nothing but my present mission could have induced me to do so. There are wheels within wheels which have made it appear that I am your enemy. But that is far from being the truth, as my present mission to you will prove."

Dora was clever and played her cards cleverly. However, Eva was on guard.

"Please come to the point," she insisted. "Tell me exactly why you have come."

Dora paused a moment, then replied, impressively, "I have come to save your father's life."

Eva caught herself almost gasping in astonishment as Dora covertly watched the effect of her words. "You have the antidote, then?" asked Eva, breathlessly.

"Not exactly that," replied Dora, quickly. "But I can take you where you can obtain it. A man has arrived from Madagascar who has it in his possession."

"What shall I do?" almost wailed the poor girl. "How can I know that you speak the truth?"

Dora's voice now assumed a cold decisiveness. "That is for you to decide," she said merely. "Refuse to come with me and your father will surely die of his madness. Consent— and he may live."

Eva could hesitate no longer. Bidding Dora wait, she ran up the stairs, returning in a few moments garbed for the street.

They left the house together, but not before the butler had surreptitiously slipped a large automatic into Eva's hand- bag.

In the Chinese temple, or Joss-house, the last devotee had departed. The hanging lights had been dimmed and now the fantastic shapes with which the place was decorated, seen in the subdued light, stood out in all their shadowy weirdness.

From the raised dais, the seven-handed god assumed an added majesty and awfulness, while, deep-seated as though from a smoldering caldron, two points of fire gleamed from the god's eyes with utmost malevolence.

Slowly a panel in the wall slid back and the bestial visage of the Strangler peered out.

After making sure that there was no one about, with noiseless tread he glided into the temple.

Like a shadow, a second figure, that of a Chinaman, followed him. The two made a complete circuit of the temple, stopping now and again to examine some object which arrested their attention. Then, as if by a prearranged signal, they both prostrated themselves before the fire god.

After making many obeisances they got to their feet and, as mysteriously as they entered, slipped away in the same manner that they had come. A panel closed behind them, but not the same panel.

The inner room in which they now found themselves was divided by a partition that extended a few feet out into the temple room itself.

This room was vividly painted with weird figures depicting Chinese forms of torture, a veritable charnel-house of what in Europe would be called the Dark Ages. There were plenty of evidences that at no very distant date this chamber had been in use to punish horribly those who had offended against the fire god or the commands of the Tong leaders.

On one side of the partition was a large iron wheel to which was attached a rope extending through the partition and forming a loop or noose on the other side. The purpose of this device was only too apparent. Once the neck of a victim was in the noose, a few turns of the wheel, the noose would tighten, and the victim would be inevitably strangled to death. In a slightly changed form it was the garroting-machine of old Spain.

The Strangler tested the rope, twisted the wheel, while his companion occupied himself by watching the effect of the wheel on the noose on the other side of the partition.

Apparently satisfied that the machine was in good working order, the Madagascan straightened up and waved his companion out of the room.

The Chinaman returned by means of the sliding panel into the temple again.

As she left Brent Rock behind, Eva's fears increased. Speeding through the night with this woman whom she instinctively dreaded, whom she had every reason to distrust, many times on the trip Eva wished herself back at her home.

On the other hand, to remain inactive while there was a chance to save her father's life was unthinkable. And so, for his sake, she kept on and the car sped ahead.

Dora, on the contrary, anxious to allay Eva's fears, was very voluble, expressing many sentiments which even to a young girl of little worldly experience were palpably at variance with the woman's character.

In and out of the narrow streets of the city's lower quarter the car twisted and turned, and at last entered gaily decked Chinatown, where it came to a halt.

If Eva was afraid before she was now doubly so. The strange Oriental faces which seemed to leer at her from street and curb seemed to be almost of another world, and she thought of the many tales she had heard, of their treachery and cunning.

Dora, sensing what was passing through her mind, kept up

a patter of small talk as she urged Eva forward.

By another entrance than the one that led through the Chinese curio-shop they entered the Joss-house and came to the worshiping-room of the temple.

Eva gazed fearfully about her now at all the fantastic decorations with which she was surrounded. Her only comfort was the handle of the automatic that the butler had pressed on her as she was leaving home.

"This Madagascan with the antidote," asked Eva, tremulously, "where is he?"

"Don't worry, dearie," quieted Dora. "Wait a moment here and I will bring him."

Dora turned on her heel and left the temple by the door leading into the beautiful lounging-room beyond.

Eva stood transfixed by the solemn awfulness of the place and the grim visage of the fire god. Why had she been brought to such a place? What new terrors awaited her here?

She seemed alone—yet was she?

She felt a thousand eyes regarding her, as though a thousand dangers lurked to destroy her just beyond those fearful walls.

She was staring now at the god. What made his eyes gleam so banefully?

She thought she heard a sound!

Was the wall at the right of the statue moving? Or was it merely her heightened imagination?

Fascinated, she watched.

Yes, she was sure now. Slowly, slowly a portion of that wall was actually sliding back.

Now she saw a hand. Then an arm followed. With a slow, gliding movement that even to Eva's strained ears was noiseless, a man, his back toward her, slid into the room.

Eva, shrinking back, wanted to shriek. But instead she whipped out the automatic and in an instant had the man covered.

The man was still evidently unconscious of her presence. But suddenly he must have heard Eva move. For he wheeled around, and instinctively his hands went above his head.

As for Eva, the cry that she had suppressed at his appearance was suppressed no longer, for the man whom she held at her mercy was—Locke!

"How did you come here?" gasped Eva.

Hurriedly he told her his story—how he felt that the clue that would lead to the unraveling of this mystery was now to be found in Chinatown, how he had made his way, therefore, to the Chinese quarter, how he had tracked the Madagascan.

Knowing the futility of trying to enter any private place of the Orientals, much less their temple, in Occidental garb, he had waylaid a Chinaman in an alley, had stripped him, and had changed clothes with him.

Disguised thus, Locke had managed to enter, to observe, and was only now on his way to summon assistance. For he had decided to have the place raided. Only now he was stricken almost dumb with astonishment at being confronted by Eva.

There was no time for more. Before Eva could explain her own presence there the door burst open, the panels slid back, and a horde of emissaries and Chinamen swarmed about them.

Eva fired her automatic again and again, but could not stay the rush.

Locke fought with the courage of despair. But they were too many and soon bore him down.

As they carried Locke into the chamber of torture the last thing he saw was Eva surrounded by her foes, who were closing in on the poor girl.

Towering above them all, he saw the gigantic form of the Automaton.

In the torture-chamber Locke was shackled hand and foot to the partition, while the noose of the garroting-machine was placed about his neck.

The Madagascan supervised this work, then waved the emissaries out of the room. They were alone there now, these two—the professional murderer and his victim.

With a sneer the Madagascan turned and went to the other side of the partition where the wheel was by which the noose was tightened, strangling the victim.

But the Strangler little knew with whom he had to deal, for already Locke was struggling at his shackles.

With almost incredible dexterity Locke succeeded in

loosening them, one after the other, so that, as the Madagascan started to turn the wheel, Locke, with a marvelous effort, bracing his feet against the wall and grasping the staples to which the shackles had been attached, managed to pin-wheel his body around and around, as the Strangler turned the iron wheel that tightened the noose which was to stifle out his life.

Fortunately the Madagascan turned slowly, so that Locke managed to turn his body faster than the wheel was being turned, thus gaining on the noose and at each revolution loosening it a trifle.

Another quick turn of his body, the pressure against his neck had become less!

Yet another complete circle, and, tearing at the noose, he managed to get his head free.

It was the work of only an instant to dash around the partition and beat the Strangler to the floor. Another instant, and he had torn back the panel into the temple.

The sight that confronted him was sickening.

Two fiends were holding Eva close to the floor, while now from the fire god's eyes a blinding glare of flame blazed forth, the two rays converging and scorching the very ground as they traveled slowly nearer and nearer, in their fatal focus, to the helpless girl.

With a wild shout, Locke charged on them all.

Taken by surprise, the brutes holding Eva were easy to handle, for the others had gone.

Fortunately, the automatic which Eva had been carrying was

lying, neglected, on the floor. Locke snatched it up and, shooting one of the thugs, managed to cower the other.

Half supporting Eva, he retreated through the torture-chamber into an outer room. There was no time to lose. Already the alarm had been spread to the other emissaries and Chinamen, and it was only a matter of seconds when all the murderous crew would again be piling after them.

Locke looked about in desperation. There was a window. He flung it open. Below, the air-shaft or court was blind. But there was a balcony by which he could reach an adjoining low roof. He had no idea where it might lead, but any unknown danger was preferable to the known dangers that threatened behind him.

Through the window he passed with Eva, and so across balconies and roofs until they came to a fire-escape, which they descended.

In another moment they were free of Chinatown.

Many a curious glance was cast at them, a young girl, well gowned, and a disheveled white man in Chinese garb.

Locke hailed a night-hawk cabman and they were soon speeding on their way back to safety and Brent Rock.

CHAPTER XXI

At the cove fishing-village, set on the extreme outskirts of the town, there stood an old fisherman's shack that was shunned by all the good folk of the city.

While there was nothing definite that could be said of the evil deeds of the inhabitants, there was much shaking of heads and wagging of tongues to the effect that all was not as it should be at the cove.

The owner of the old shack, Old Tom, was an ill-favored, taciturn man who would have naught to do with any of his neighbors, and asked only that they keep out of his path and leave him alone. He even evinced an aversion to dogs and to little children, driving them away from his shack whenever he found them near it.

The threat that "Old Tom will catch you" would make a cove fishing-village tractable at any time.

Old Tom rarely put to sea, and when he did it was more often than not after nightfall, a time when the good folk of the village were preparing for a night's rest.

It was stated by one old crony that often at night other men came to Old Tom's shack, that they entered slyly, and that well into the morning revelry, and often oaths and brawls, could be heard from within.

Some hinted that Old Tom was a smuggler; others, even, that he was a wrecker. True it was that often strange lights were seen to flicker outside the bar to the cove.

Also there had been wrecks, and often, in the morning, when the fishermen put out to a wreck, after a storm, it would be discovered that some one had been there before them, since valuable and readily portable parts of the wreck were frequently missing.

But while suspicion pointed to Old Tom and the strange men that frequented his place, proofs positive of a crime were invariably lacking, and so the village tolerated Old Tom's presence and predicted his bad end.

It was to this shack that there came very early one morning, before the break of day, a wounded man assisted by a woman. The woman gave a peculiar rap at the door. There was a quick scurry inside, as of fast-moving feet, then silence.

The woman rapped again, and this time with more force. After a moment a sash was raised and a querulous voice demanded what was wanted.

"It's De Luxe Dora and Paul Balcom, and he's wounded. Quick, open the door!"

There was a rush to open the door now and rough hands gently assisted the wounded man to a seat inside.

While Paul was not perhaps so dangerously wounded, yet it was easy to be seen that the wound was not to be trifled with, for the cut had been severe and the blood flowed copiously.

Dora, whatever her attitude toward others, had a true solicitude for Paul, and all the womanliness of her nature came to the surface as she tenderly bathed Paul's head and attempted to bind the wound with the rough bandages at hand.

There were several tough-looking men standing about, and from their ready sympathy, real or feigned, it was easy to be seen that these men, too, like the others of the underworld, stood ready to do Paul's slightest bidding, to guard him with their lives if need be.

What was this strange power that this man, scarcely more than a youth, wielded over these outlawed men?

"Quick!" exclaimed Dora. "Watch the window. We've probably been followed."

A grim-visaged man moved lumberingly over to the window and glued his head against the pane, straining his eyes as he peered out.

For a long time he did not move, while, with the others grouped around, Dora tried to stanch the flow of blood from Paul's injured head.

Suddenly the watcher at the window turned and shouted, "Man comin' up the lane!"

Instantly there was confusion within the shack. The men scattered in all directions, while one old hag, the only woman in the shack besides Dora, hobbled over to a stool and took up the mending of a huge net where she had left off.

Old Tom ambled over to Dora and for a moment they talked hurriedly. Finally Dora came to a decision, as she

Arthur B. Reeve and John W. Grey

pointed to the old rickety stairway to an attic above.

"Carry him to the attic," she directed. "He can be well hidden there. As for the rest of you, remember, no one has come here to-night."

Two of the men lifted Paul, who, while not in an absolutely unconscious condition, was much too weak by this time from loss of blood to assist himself.

They carried him up the stairs and into an old, disused room to which Dora followed, and when the two men had descended the stairs she remained, alternately ministering to Paul and listening for what might happen below.

Paul and Dora had left the main room of the shack not a moment too soon. For barely had the two men who had carried Paul to the attic returned when a face was momentarily seen outside, while a pair of eyes peered into the room.

A moment later there was a peremptory knock at the door.

"Come in!" growled Old Tom.

With eyes that scanned every cranny and nook and searched every face, Locke stepped into the shack.

The men came forward a step, then halted. There was something in Locke's face that showed that he was in deadly earnest and not to be trifled with.

Locke looked from one to the other, then turned to Old Tom. "The wounded man who was brought here," he demanded, "where is he?"

"There 'ain't been no wounded man brought here," retorted Old Tom.

The men crowded a little closer, all denying vehemently that any one had entered.

At this instant a drop of blood fell on Locke's sleeve from the ceiling above. Quickly he checked the impulse to look up, although he was startled by it. He recovered himself on the instant and waited until under a pretext he could divert their attention to something else. Then he glanced hastily upward, as they looked in another direction. There, forming slowly, was another drop of blood, and it was about to fall.

Locke had gained his object. As surely as though he had been brought face to face with Paul, he knew that he was lying on the floor of the attic above.

Single-handed, against so many and in this shack, Locke realized that he could do nothing. He apologized gruffly for his intrusion, conveying the impression that he felt he had made a mistake, and backed his way to the door.

In an instant the door to the attic stairs was flung open and Dora rushed into the room.

"You fools!" she snarled at the surprised men who were just congratulating themselves on how they had put one over on Locke. "I tell you he's wise. He saw the blood. Look up above you. Now go get him."

But the fishermen had no desire for this outside work and hung back, while Dora raved at them.

From the ceiling, drop by drop, blood was falling, forming a little pool on the floor. Paul could not be moved now. They must make the best of it and be ready for any raid Locke might prepare.

At Brent Rock Eva was conversing with her lawyer. Matters

had reached such a state in the affairs of International Patents that it was evident, even to her, that some drastic action must be taken, and at once.

In a corner of the room, coiled up in a big armchair, Zita was apparently reading a new magazine, but was, in reality, listening intently to every word that was being uttered.

Finally Eva and the lawyer were in full accord, and she accompanied the elderly attorney to the door. As they parted, Zita strained her ears to hear the last words. She did not get it all, but quite enough to tell her what they had decided upon.

"As my lawyer," she overheard Eva say, "I wish you to have Mr. Locke appointed receiver."

There was some more she missed, but that was quite enough for Zita. She got out of the chair quickly and left the room without being observed, and a few moments later she had left the house.

In a telephone-booth, not far from the cove fishing-village, Locke by this time had his chief of the Department of Justice on the wire.

"I've located him, Chief," he telephoned, excitedly, "but it will take four good men to capture him."

"I'll send them at once," the chief replied, as both hung up their receivers hurriedly.

Meanwhile, in Herbert Balcom's sumptuous, semi-Oriental apartment two men were in earnest conversation. One was the owner, Balcom, the other that strange, half-demented being, Doctor Q, whose mind now, for the moment, seemed to be lucid.

The matter under discussion was undoubtedly a weighty one, for both men sat with knitted brows, and for the moment, at least, seemed in a quandary about something.

Suddenly there came a hurried ringing at the outside-door bell and Balcom leaped to his feet. They could hear the door opened, quick footsteps in the hallway, and then, without ceremony, the door was flung open and Dora burst into the room.

Balcom scowled a welcome, for he hated this woman, who had, as he thought, spoiled the chances of his son with Eva. But Dora did not wait for the threatened outburst.

"Hurry!" she cried. "You must do something. Paul has been wounded—never mind how—but he lies in a fishing-shack down at the cove—and they are going to arrest him— Locke is!"

For the moment both men seemed to be stricken dumb, while Dora, in a state of wild excitement, pleaded for them to do something—anything to save the one person she loved.

It was at this juncture that the door opened again, admitting another woman. It was Zita, very agitated, though, of course, under better control than Dora. Besides, Zita did not know what had happened to Paul, nor did she love him. It was merely that she felt that things could be made to play into her own hands if the news she brought were immediately acted upon.

Hastily she told what she had overheard about the proposed receivership, and all four now—Balcom, Doctor Q, Dora, and Zita—talked excitedly.

But it was plainly Balcom who was in command of the

Arthur B. Reeve and John W. Grey

situation. Although livid with rage at the news he had heard, yet he maintained control of the others, directing what they should do with a decisiveness that was truly remarkable. It showed the mental force of the man, demonstrating how greatly he was to be feared by any bold enough to be his enemy. For Balcom loved that spoiled son of his and would hesitate at no act, not even at a crime, to save him from even what he justly deserved.

At last their plan was formed, and all four departed their several ways to execute it.

Balcom had decided upon going directly to Brent Rock. His ire had not abated one iota during the trip, either, and, as he almost ran up the steps to the mansion, he pushed the astounded butler to one side as though he were merely a piece of furniture.

"Tell Miss Brent I want to see her at once," he threatened.

The butler raised a hand deprecatingly at Balcom's tone, but Balcom, beside himself, smashed it down and strode toward the library just as Eva, hearing the voices, was coming out. For an instant she drew back in apprehension and amazement as Balcom advanced on her, still snarling.

"See here, Eva," he hissed, "if Locke tries to arrest my son— he'll be killed."

For the instant Eva was stunned. What did the man mean? But as Balcom showed no signs of regaining control of himself, and every moment became more abusive and violent, indignation gave place to every other sentiment, and she sharply ordered Balcom to leave the house.

Threatening dire things and hinting even more if there were a receivership, Balcom strode out.

Eva stood for a long time shocked into inaction. Then, slowly, fears for Locke's safety came uppermost and she paced back and forth the length of the hall.

Finally the old butler came to her deferentially.

"And did you notice, ma'am," he asked, "that during his tirade he mentioned about a cove fishing-village? Might I suggest that that is where Mr. Paul is and Mr. Locke will not be found far off?"

Eva thought a moment, recognized the sound sense of the remark, and ordered that her car be brought. A few moments later she had taken the wheel and was soon out of sight of Brent Rock.

Close pressed against a wall of a back lane of the cove fishing-village, Locke was standing, waiting for the men whom his chief had promised to send.

Finally they came to him, first making their coming known to Locke by a peculiar low whistle.

"The other two will be along directly," whispered one of the pair. "Thought it better not to come in a bunch."

As Locke laid his plans, the other two came from out of the shadows.

The entire party now moved cautiously toward Old Tom's shack. Just before they arrived one of the men said that he could see two figures entering the place. But as Locke had seen nothing, no attention was paid to the remark.

Locke now placed one of his men on either side of the door. The other two he sent to the rear, so that they could surround the gang.

Arthur B. Reeve and John W. Grey

He knocked at the door. This time it was immediately opened. Followed by the detectives with revolvers drawn, Locke rushed boldly into the shack, while his other two men closed in from the rear.

The emissaries, finding themselves surrounded, would have capitulated, probably without a struggle, had not the old hag, to whom no one had paid much attention, picked up a small anchor and thrown it at Locke and the advancing detectives.

As it was, the anchor struck Locke a glancing blow and he stumbled backward against one of his own men, upsetting him. That, of course, gave the advantage to the thugs, and they advanced, attacking savagely.

It was at too close quarters, in the midst of such a melee, to use guns without danger of getting one of one's own party. Thus it was a primitive battle of brute force.

Locke and the detectives were trained men, however, and were surely gaining the upper hand, so much so that Locke managed to tear himself loose and dash for the door leading to the attic. He opened it, and there, with revolver leveled at his head, stood De Luxe Dora.

It was the work of only an instant to disarm her, however, and he rushed up the stairs, Dora after him.

There was a body lying on the floor—Paul, undoubtedly, thought Locke.

He took it by the shoulder and turned it over, then fell back in amazement, for there, smiling mockingly at him, was Zita!

"You think you're pretty clever, don't you?" jeered Dora.

But it was no time to bandy words, and Locke left them and rushed down the stairs just as a horde of emissaries swarmed up to meet him, reinforcements to the fisher thugs.

For in some way the Automaton had been warned of Locke's presence, and with all the emissaries it could summon had hastened to Old Tom's shack.

Most unfortunate of all, the Automaton and its men had arrived just behind the car bearing Eva, and she, not suspecting the danger, had entered the shack.

Although she did not see Locke, she was overjoyed to see that the detectives held the upper hand. She had started to search for him, when there came a terrifying crash at the door and more emissaries, followed by the Automaton, came into the room.

The detectives were almost instantly overpowered, and the mob made for the stairs just as Locke was descending.

In that narrow space a most terrible battle took place. Man after man Locke hurled against his fellows, and they went crashing down, only to rise again and attack.

Finally they came to hand-grips, and Locke, lunging furiously to free himself, threw his body against the partition of the stairway and it came crashing down, hurling Locke and the emissaries to the floor below.

Locke was badly stunned, and before he could rise the emissaries had swathed him in the huge net that the old hag had been mending. Next they bound him with ropes until he was utterly helpless in the meshes of the net.

Eva, half crazed with horror, was in a far corner, and the Automaton was advancing upon her. She was paralyzed with fear.

What fate was in store for her—what for Locke?

CHAPTER XXII

The sharp crack of an automatic echoed through the shack. The detective known as Jim had come back to consciousness, and now, from behind an overturned table where he had fallen, he started to fire shot after shot into the mob of emissaries.

He had fallen in a far corner and could be reached only after an attack of some paces, and even the emissaries, numerous as they were, hesitated to advance on a determined man placed in such an advantageous position. Furthermore, the diversion caused by the shots had other effects. The sound of the shots brought Locke fully out of his stunned condition and he started to struggle frantically in the meshes of the net that held him prisoner.

The Automaton, for the moment, ceased to follow Eva, and moved over to its men in order to take command and to direct their movements, while yet another detective came to his senses and began to threaten the mob.

Locke was threshing about and was slowly but surely freeing himself. An emissary threw a chair, and for a moment Locke lay still in pain. But in another moment he was working even more frantically at the ropes and the net that held him.

Eva started over to help him, but he shouted to her to stand

Arthur B. Reeve and John W. Grey

back, since that would bring her in line with the detectives' fire. The shots were flying over Locke's body as he struggled. Some of the emissaries went down; others found places of refuge behind which they hid.

Finally Locke managed to kick his feet free of the net and, rolling and tossing, managed to work the meshes up about his shoulders and neck, thus releasing his hands. It was the work of an instant only, now, to slip the enveloping net over his head and he was free.

Locke rolled out of the direction of the revolver-shots and toward Eva, who was now standing before a huge open fireplace.

He was none too soon, for the moment that the Automaton saw that Locke had escaped the iron terror left the men and stalked ponderously over to crush out Locke's life.

The two detectives fired point-blank at the monster and both shots took effect with a ringing, metallic sound. But they did not halt the Automaton an instant. Locke, reaching the fireplace, seized a pair of old tongs and threw firebrand after firebrand in the path of the advancing terror.

To the Automaton fire was evidently quite another affair from mere puny bullets, for it not only paused, but came to a full stop, looking around as though in a quandary as to what to do against such a defense.

This moment of hesitation gave Locke and Eva their opportunity. Calling to the detectives to cease firing a moment, they passed between friends and foes, dashed over to and up the attic stairs.

As they reached the attic above they were just in time to see Zita, still dressed in Paul's clothes, and Dora, jump from the attic window.

Although it was a low, rambling building, still it was a high jump, even for a man, and Locke was astounded that they should attempt such a thing, even in their undoubted state of panic.

However, it gave Locke a splendid idea, which he acted upon immediately. Hooking his feet on the window-frame, he took hold of Eva's wrists firmly and swung her far out of the window. Held in this way, Eva was only a few feet from the ground, and when Locke released her she landed safely and almost without a jar.

For Locke, always in perfect training, the jump offered no difficulties. In an instant he had rejoined her and they were running away from the shack toward Eva's waiting car.

Locke had an almost overpowering desire to return to assist his detectives, whom he realized might be in sore straits, but he also realized that his first duty was to this girl who was in his charge, on whom the events through which they had just passed had had a nerve-racking effect. Again, he reflected, as he saw people coming down the beach, that the Automaton and his men would soon be outnumbered and glad to flee.

Quentin and Eva had almost reached the motor which Eva had left at some distance from Old Tom's shack, and were passing a low clump of bushes, when a low moan fell upon their ears.

At first Locke thought that it might be a trap and was for paying no attention to the sound, but Eva, woman-like, insisted. He investigated. Reclining on the ground, and looking more like a little boy in man's clothes, lay Zita.

She was holding one ankle and her face showed that she

must be in great pain.

"Help me," she moaned. "When I jumped from the window I sprained my ankle. Dora helped me to this place and then she left me and drove away."

Although this girl was his enemy, no thought of leaving her in this condition entered Locke's mind. Gently raising her from the ground, with the help of Eva, Locke supported her to the car.

Locke still held Zita to ease her pain, while Eva took the wheel, and, although they could hear shouts and even shots behind them, Eva drove slowly in order not to add to Zita's misery. It showed the sympathy of their characters that, much as Locke and Eva felt that Zita had injured them, nevertheless, pausing in a flight from deadly peril, they found it in their hearts to be kind to an enemy.

Arriving at Brent Rock, they carried Zita to her room and the family physician was sent for. He pronounced the injury slight and more of a strain than a sprain.

While the doctor was at the house he also paid a visit to Brent, who, while his mental condition had remained as apparently hopeless as ever, had gained much in strength, owing to the diet and restful care. He was now able to sit up, fully dressed. As it was a case of drug poisoning, the doctor had thought it best not to allow the patient to relax too completely. But, whatever the strange drug that had stolen away Brent's reason, the effect showed no signs of departure, and they were as much in the dark as to the antidote as ever.

A few moments after the doctor had left, when he made his morning call the next day, the counsel of the corporation was announced. He was shown into the library immediately and it was there that Locke and Eva went into conference with him.

The attorney had brought with him many share-holders' proxies, and these he handed over to Eva.

"These proxies," he was declaring, "give you absolute control, Miss Brent. With them you can force Mr. Balcom completely out of International Patents."

"What's that you say?"

It was Balcom himself who spoke. How the man had got past the butler, who certainly had no love for him, was mystifying. Yet here he was, ready and eager to defend his interests.

"I was just telling Miss Brent," informed the lawyer, coldly, "that with these proxies which I have obtained and just handed to her, she was in complete control of the company."

"And you, Mr. Balcom," interposed Locke, stepping forward, "will play no further part in the activities of the company. Miss Brent desires your resignation, to take effect immediately."

"Why—why—this is unheard of—absurd!" sputtered Balcom. "I'll—I'll—" And his rage got the better of him.

"No, Mr. Balcom," again interrupted Locke, "you will do nothing. It is I who will give you twenty-four hours to arrange your affairs with the company before I order your removal—or arrest."

Balcom tried to remonstrate, to plead his innocence of any wrong-doing. Finding no sympathy by taking this attitude, his manner changed abruptly and he attempted to bluster.

A decisive movement toward the telephone on the part of Locke checked this and, chameleon-like, Balcom's usual suave manner came to the fore. He bowed himself out.

"It will, of course, be as you say." He smiled oilily.

Once in the hall, however, his manner changed again, and, darkly scowling and biting his thin lips, he was about to quit the place, when Zita, limping only slightly, intercepted him.

"Mr. Balcom," she pleaded, "come out the back way. I must see you alone a moment."

They tiptoed out to the grounds, and, behind a hedge where they could not be observed from the house, talked.

"Tell me what has happened," demanded Zita.

"Happened?" repeated Balcom. "Why, they've thrown me out of the company—at least, they think they have."

His mind was working quickly, and after a pause he turned to Zita sharply. "Can you get Brent out of the house and bring him to me here behind this hedge at eight o'clock to-night?"

Zita nodded an eager acquiescence and left him, returning to the house.

That evening Locke, returning from a stroll around the grounds, noticed a movement in some shrubbery at the side of the foot-path. He went closer to investigate, and a rough-looking individual broke from cover and ran away through the underbrush as fast as he could go. It was too dark to follow and Locke hastened his steps to the house, fearing some new deviltry on the part of the Automaton or his emissaries.

He had just entered the darkened hallway when, much to his surprise, he saw the figure of a man, leaning heavily on the arm of a woman, descending the stairs.

He stepped behind some portieres and waited until they reached the foot of the stairway. Then he stepped out and confronted them.

Zita gave a startled cry, and would have fled had not Locke caught and held her. As for poor Brent, he simply stood there, swaying from side to side and smiling foolishly.

Eva heard the commotion and came running down the stairs. She was amazed until Locke explained the situation to her. Then her indignation knew no bounds. Putting her arms around her father, she turned to Zita.

"How dare you?" she demanded, scathingly. "For doing this you will leave this house immediately and—never return."

Zita, for a moment, was on the verge of breaking down, but recovered herself and, with an angry retort on her lips, went out, slamming the door behind her.

Zita slipped around the house and to the hedge designated by Balcom as their meeting-place.

She was surprised but relieved when she did not find him there, and glanced at her wrist watch, which stood at a few minutes past eight. She was about to turn around when she caught sight of a bit of paper. Taking it, she read:

Bring him to my rooms.

That was all, and the message was unsigned.

Zita greatly feared Balcom's wrath at her failure, but, nevertheless, she started for his apartment.

At that moment Balcom and the mysterious Doctor Q were talking in the latter's dingy laboratory. Doctor Q's mind, for the time being, at least, seemed perfectly clear, and he had formulated a daring plan.

"Send Locke word that you will give yourself up," he was saying, "but tell him that he must come to your apartment to get you. I will do the rest."

Balcom left hurriedly and was driven directly home, where he got Locke on the telephone and repeated the instructions that Doctor Q had suggested.

"Am I to understand that you intend to turn state's evidence?" questioned Locke, doubtfully.

"Assuredly," hastened Balcom.

"Then I'll be right over."

As Balcom hung up the receiver he chuckled sardonically. He was just turning to an antique brazier to arrange for Locke's reception when Zita was announced and at once admitted.

"I've failed, Mr. Balcom," she apologized, "failed miserably. Locke took Mr. Brent away from me—and they ordered me never to return to the house."

"You little idiot!" Balcom almost hissed. "I'll not tolerate a failure, either. Get out!"

Although Zita almost went on her knees in her pleading to him, Balcom was adamant, and finally she left in utter despair.

Outside, she telephoned to Paul to see if she might induce him to use his influence in reinstating her in his father's good graces.

As soon as Zita was gone Balcom busied himself with the ancient brazier and was standing before a small image of Buddha. He took a small package and from it poured a powder into the bowl of the brazier. Then, going to the table, he wrote a short note, after which he went to a divan and awaited Locke's coming.

Balcom had not long to wait. A ring came at the door and Balcom leaped to his feet and lighted the powder in the brazier. Then he adjusted a gas-mask that Doctor Q had given him, and, returning to the divan, lay down, pulling a camel's-hair coverlet well over himself as he awaited results.

There was a rap at the door and a peremptory demand for entrance—a pause—and a whispered consultation outside.

"Open the door!" cried Locke, again.

As there was no answer, heavy blows were rained upon the door, and finally it gave way.

Three men stumbled into the room. They stared about, then started to search the place. One by one they started to cough. Locke, who was the farthest away from the brazier, seemed to be the least affected.

Finally he spied the note on the table and snatched it up. By the dim light he read:

You will never live to capture me. The deadly gas is even now killing you.

Locke gasped. There was the sound of a heavy fall behind him. He turned and saw that one of his men was down.

He took a step forward, when the other pitched on his face.

Locke tried to rescue them, but by this time the deadly fumes had reached him and he, too, fell to the floor, coughing his life away.

At that moment Balcom got up from the divan and, stepping over Locke's prostrate body, left the place, forgetting to close the door behind him.

When Zita telephoned Paul, Paul made an immediate appointment for her to meet him at Doctor Q's, and when she arrived there Paul was already in conference with the doctor.

Over the telephone Zita had already given Paul a brief account of what had happened, and thus the two men were prepared with a plan when she arrived.

"Get Eva to the hypnotist's on River Street," instructed Doctor Q. "Tell her that I have been hypnotized and that under the spell I will tell all."

It was a desperate thing for Zita to attempt, after treating the Brents so shamelessly. But there was no alternative. For she knew well that, with Balcom, only a success would offset her miserable failure earlier in the evening. Besides, were not her fortunes tied up with Balcom—or perhaps with Paul? She did not demur, but left immediately for Brent Rock to make the attempt, revolving in her mind how she was to do it.

Zita had difficulty in persuading Eva to see her at all, but, once she had succeeded, the possibility that all the mystery might be cleared up appealed strongly to Eva. For Zita had framed her story cleverly and was playing desperately.

"Then I'll meet you at the hypnotist's in about half an hour," agreed Eva, after Zita had told her how friendless she herself was and how both Balcom and Paul had refused her aid.

Zita left Brent Rock alone and was passing a dark corner when a hand reached out and grasped her by the arm and she heard a voice that she recognized.

"Your failure has made me redouble my efforts," it hissed. "I have just killed Locke in my apartment and I—"

It was Balcom. But Zita waited to hear no more. Secretly she had always loved Locke. Though she had worked against him, the very thought that he might be dead shocked her. She tore herself from the grasp of Balcom before she could hear more and ran like a deer toward the apartment.

Fortunately, it was not far. She tore up-stairs and through the door that Balcom had left open.

Everything was as Balcom had left it, except that now the three men lay quite still. Zita staggered over to a window and threw it open.

Next she got water and extinguished the still smoldering powder. Then, falling on her knees, she tried to help the stricken men.

Not much time did she spend with the others, but to Locke with great tenderness she gave most of her attention. Tenderly she bathed his brow and frantically tried even to

Arthur B. Reeve and John W. Grey

breathe her breath into his burning lungs.

Finally she was rewarded by seeing him open his eyes and gaze around. He looked up at her.

"I'll atone for all the wrong I've done," she sobbed, "only—"

She would have asked him to love her, but she knew that it was useless and the thought of Eva, caused the words to stick in her throat.

Locke did not understand, and the look on his face showed it.

"I didn't want to give you up," wailed Zita, now forgetting herself. "I loved you. To prove it—I will help you now. The—the girl you love is in terrible danger—you must hurry."

It was only too true. Eva had driven immediately to the hypnotist's, and he had been instructed about her coming. At his door she had knocked, and an old, evil-visaged man, in flowing robes which were marked in cabalistic signs, had opened the door. In true fakir fashion he salaamed almost to the floor while in flowery language he bade her enter.

Fearfully Eva stepped within. Signs of the zodiac, of cross-bones and skulls, on walls and ceiling met her gaze everywhere. In an alcove Eva could see a noosed rope hanging, for what purpose she knew not. But its presence she felt was sinister.

"I—I was told that a Doctor Q would be here," Eva faltered. "I do not see him."

"Gracious lady," bowed the hyponotist, "I will bring him at

once. Pray be seated."

Eva seated herself before a table upon which there stood a curious stand, supporting many mirrors. She examined it closely, and as she did so they all began to move. Each mirror moved on its own axis and she watched with fatal curiosity. For now a bright light was cast from behind her on the revolving mirrors and they formed a scintillating kaleidoscope that was bewildering in its intricacy.

Eva quickly became fascinated. Then she was conscious of a drowsy feeling stealing over her. She strove to rise, but her knees refused to support her and she fell back in her chair.

The hypnotist now shut off the machine and, stepping before Eva, made several passes with his hands.

Eva's eyes closed. The hypnotist turned and made a signal. Several panels opened simultaneously and into the room there came a number of emissaries, who crept upon the now completely hypnotized girl.

Nor was that all. A sound, as of the clanking of chains, was heard, and through an aperture in the wall larger than the others there stalked the Automaton.

At this very instant Locke and Zita burst into the room and rushed toward Eva.

The hypnotist slipped around them both and in a moment had caught Zita in his arms. She struggled to escape, beating him with her little fists in a fury of rage and fear. But he held her, and an emissary, bringing ropes, with his help bound her securely.

As for Locke, he made a frantic attempt to reach Eva, but his way was blocked by a score of emissaries and the

Automaton himself. Desperately Locke dashed at the iron monster, only to be hurled to the floor as though he were a tiny child.

In another moment the emissaries had bound him and carried him to the alcove in which hung the noosed rope.

The hypnotist now pulled a lever and the method of the death intended for Locke was revealed. Directly under the suspended rope was a trap-door, which opened. Locke gazed down into blackness, nothingness. An emissary threw some small, heavy object into the yawning hole. For a long time nothing was heard. Then finally, far, far below there came to their ears the sound of a distant splash.

The fiendish plan was simple—to hang him and then to cut the rope. His body would go hurtling down to the subterranean river below and be carried out to sea.

The hypnotist reversed the lever. The trap-door closed. Locke was dragged beneath the rope and it was adjusted around his neck.

Even in this awful moment his sole thought was of Eva. Would they throw her, unconscious, down the same yawning trap?

Powerless, he stood bound, fascinated, as he saw three emissaries seize her. But instead of dragging her to the trap, they dragged her toward one of the panels in the wall.

What nameless torture was in store for her?

He struggled furiously to get free to rush to her, but the noose only tightened on his neck.

The hypnotist stepped to the lever that operated the trap under Locke's feet and began to pull the lever down.

Arthur B. Reeve and John W. Grey

CHAPTER XXIII

With a crash the hypnotist dropped unconscious to the floor as the hypnotic machine started to revolve rapidly. The emissaries turned from Locke and were dazzled by the blinding flashes from the whirling mirrors.

It was Zita who caused all the commotion. Unnoticed by the thugs, who were intent on sending Locke to his death and dragging Eva through the panel, Zita had managed to free herself from her bonds and, true to her promise to Locke that she would help him, she had risked all for his sake.

Once free from the ropes, she had seized a heavy bronze vase and, at just the critical moment of danger, had hurled it at the hypnotist's head, striking him a terrific blow that had felled him and left him unconscious on the floor before he could spring the trap. She had then set the mechanical hypnotic machine in motion, and, standing behind it, was herself practically invisible. It all happened so quickly that it seemed like a miracle.

Locke, his hope revived, swiftly grasped the one chance for life that was left to him. By contracting his muscles he was able to slip out of the ropes which bound his arms. But since the noosed rope around his neck held him so that his toes barely touched the floor of the trap, he could not, try as he might, manage to get the noose free.

Suddenly a plan flashed across his mind. Hanging from the ceiling a few feet in front of him he could see an enormous chandelier. Throwing his hands above his head, he grasped the rope, thus relieving the strain on his neck. Then, snapping his body backward, his feet came in contact with the wall. With tremendous force he kicked out, causing his body to swing in an arc toward the chandelier.

It was not until he had wrapped his legs about the branches of the chandelier that the emissaries noticed what he was doing, so fascinated were they by the revolving mirrors. Even then they could scarcely resist the auto-hypnotic powers of the contrivance. Finally, however, with a shout they came to the attack.

Locke was now hanging head downward. With one hand he succeeded in loosening the noose from about his neck, while with the other he struck out, hitting an emissary a fearful swinging blow that sent the fellow staggering backward, to fall against the lever controlling the trap-door.

With a crash the trap was sprung, with the pit yawning beneath it. Struggling, striking, grappling with his assailants, Locke managed to hurl three of them to their deaths in the underground river below.

Horror-stricken at the fate of their companions, the other emissaries stepped back, when, to add to their confusion, Zita, with remarkable strength for so frail a girl, lifted the stand of mirrors and hurled it among them.

Locke somersaulted to the floor and, seizing the broken stand, used it as a weapon with deadly effect.

The emissaries turned and fled.

An instant later Locke started to the panel through which Eva had been dragged, when he heard steps from the other side. It was the emissaries who had seized Eva, coming back to see what all the rumpus was about. Locke, forewarned, slipped close to the wall, and, as they passed through the panel, one at a time, he was able to fell them to the floor.

Then he rushed through the panel just in time to see Eva, pursued by the Automaton, running toward him.

The very strangeness of her terrible adventure had brought Eva out of the hypnotic state into which she had been thrown and she clung to Locke as though she were a child.

Locke took her in his arms and, swiftly evading the slow-moving monster, dashed back to the hypnotic room, calling to Zita to run to the street. Thus all three were able to make good their escape.

Eva had purposely left her motor turning over, and therefore it was barely an instant after they were in the street before they were streaking out of that quarter of the town.

Zita was now overwhelmed by her feelings, but it was Eva herself who spoke first.

"Forgive me, Zita," begged Eva, in the rush of her emotions forgetting all that Zita had done. "But for you, both of us would now be dead."

For some moments Zita could not reply in her silent sadness at seeing the joy of Locke with this girl.

"I—I forgive you?" she murmured, at length. "It is for you to forgive me." She paused a moment and choked back a sob; then added, bravely, "I—I can even wish for your happiness, my dear; my hope is dead."

Only Locke understood, and as he watched Zita he resolved to do all he could for her, realizing that some one else had made her a victim of her love and jealousy.

All breathed a sigh of relief when at last they came again in sight of the lights of Brent Rock.

There was just the trace of a shadow to cloud the momentary happiness at their safe arrival, as, on the steps, Zita refused to enter.

"I—I must say good-by," she murmured, wistfully, turning to go out into the night alone.

Nothing that either Locke or Eva could say seemed to swerve her purpose.

"Can't you see?" she exclaimed, finally, turning to Locke. "Balcom, Paul, and Doctor Q all trust me now. I can help you solve the mystery better if I leave the house."

This was so evident that Locke and Eva were forced to consent. They took her back to the city, leaving her where she could be unobserved, then returned in a very hopeful mood again to Brent Rock.

"I think she can and will help us," declared Eva, intuitively.

"Yes," agreed Locke, slowly, "and if Zita finds the record of her birth I believe we shall solve the mystery."

Worn out with the terrors through which she had passed, Eva bade Locke an affectionate good-night and went to her room, while he went to the laboratory and tried again to find an antidote for the Madagascar madness, a work that kept him up late and to which he returned again early the following morning.

Arthur B. Reeve and John W. Grey

It was on that following day, in the River Road apartment of De Luxe Dora, that Paul and she were having a demi-monde lovers' quarrel. Paul was intoxicated, and Dora may have been angry about that. Or it may have been that she was jealous of some other woman. However, they were quarreling fiercely when there came a knock at the door.

"You open it," flashed Dora to Paul.

He demurred a moment, then, changing his mind, consented and crossed to the door, while Dora ran to her own room and hid.

Paul was very much surprised to find that the visitor was Zita, much excited.

"I want you to help me on something of great importance," she exclaimed, almost before she had entered.

"Why, certainly! Anything you desire!" hiccoughed Paul. "Come on in."

Zita entered the apartment and they crossed over to the chaise-longue, where Zita made her direct plea.

"Help me find the record of my birth," she begged.

Paul pulled his wandering wits together and thought a moment; then a particularly crafty look came into his eyes as he detached a key from his key-ring.

"Here, take this," he directed. "It's the key to my father's apartment. The records you want are there. He and I have quarreled and you can go as far as you like."

Zita took the key eagerly, thanked Paul profusely, and started for the door.

She had barely passed the threshold before Dora, who had heard all, was at the telephone in her own room and was angrily calling up Balcom at his apartment.

Balcom, assisted by his Madagascan servant, was at the moment packing a trunk, perhaps preparatory to a hasty flight, should that become necessary. The moment the telephone rang he picked up the receiver and nearly choked with anger as he heard Dora's whispered voice over the wire.

"Paul has given Zita the key to your apartment," Dora hastened, "and she is coming over to steal the record of her birth."

"She is—eh? Well, I'll take care of that," growled Balcom, as he rang off.

Balcom went to a drawer in the table and from it took a large book. Rapidly he turned over the pages until he found what he wanted. Then he made an erasure and an entry and replaced the book in the drawer. Next he called the servant.

"When she comes, you make her a prisoner," he directed. "Understand?"

The Madagascan nodded and raised one of Balcom's hands to his own forehead as a sign of his fidelity.

Balcom went out and the servant stepped into the empty trunk to await the arrival of Zita.

But it was a very different person with whom the Madagascan had to contend in the end.

On leaving Dora's apartment, Zita telephoned Brent Rock, and Locke answered immediately. Locke readily agreed to make the search of Balcom's apartment in Zita's stead.

When the Madagascan heard a key in the door he stealthily peeped from his hiding-place and saw, instead of Zita, Locke.

Locke's back was turned, and the Madagascan, undaunted, sprang from the trunk and leaped, catlike, on Locke's back. But he had not reckoned on his antagonist. Locke, always on guard, was not taken quite by surprise. He caught the savage in a jiu-jitsu hold, throwing him over his head to land in a far corner of the room.

In spite of the fall, the Madagascan bounded to his feet, like a rubber ball, but a few stiff jabs from Locke soon took all the fight out of him and he lay still, completely knocked out.

Locke made a hurried but systematic search of the room, and finally found the book that he sought, taking it and returning to Eva at Brent Rock.

After telephoning, Zita went directly to Doctor Q's laboratory, to which she was admitted after he had seen her through his periscope annunciator.

The doctor was fumbling with a test-tube, from which some heavy fumes were issuing. He motioned her to a chair, near a table upon which were many papers which looked to Zita as though they might be of importance. Always quick to act, Zita raised her hand as if to arrange her hair, and as she did so she purposely knocked the test-tube out of the doctor's hand. The acid spattered on some of the papers, quickly setting them afire.

Doctor Q, wildly excited, started to beat out the flames, and in so doing allowed several unseared letters to flutter to the floor. One in particular arrested Zita's attention. It was a drawing, a plan of some sort, and was marked, "Plan of Den."

Zita placed her foot on it, and, while Doctor Q was engaged with the small blaze, she reached down and, hastily folding it, thrust it into one of the low shoes she was wearing. Then she went to Doctor Q's assistance and in a jiffy the fire was out. The doctor was furiously angry at her, and, feeling that she had accomplished all that she might expect, she expressed her regrets for the accident and went out before his anger became any worse.

Thus it was that Zita arrived at Brent Rock only a few moments after Locke, whom she found in the library with Eva, turning over the pages of the record he had secured at Balcom's.

The record purported to be a record of marriages of Wallace County, New York, and Locke finally found an entry that read, "Peter Brent and Rita Dane."

For a moment Zita was stunned. It was her mother's name.

Locke smiled. "Yes, Zita," he said, quietly, "for a moment Eva and I were surprised, too. But it's a palpable forgery. Balcom has tried to prove that you and Eva are half-sisters, but look."

He handed her a powerful magnifying-glass and through it the clumsy forgery stood out in all its crudeness, showing plainly where other names had been erased and these inserted.

Zita was greatly disappointed, for she had thought that at last she would establish her identity. Then she remembered the paper she had hidden in her shoe. She slipped the paper out and handed it to Locke, who was greatly excited over its importance.

They were still studying it when Locke heard a strange noise, as of shuffling feet, in the hallway. He jumped to the door, and there, in the dim light of the stairway leading down to the Graveyard of Genius, he saw a knot of men carrying another man, who was evidently helpless. Locke started forward, but they were gone.

Eva hurried up-stairs to her father's room, fearing something was wrong.

"Father's gone!" she cried, despairingly.

Locke threw himself full against the door at the head of the cellar stairs which the men had slammed shut. He tried to batter it down, but it was too strongly built. Then he drew his revolver and with the barrel started to push out the pins from the hinges. He worked feverishly and succeeded in driving the top pin out. Then, using it as a lever, he was able to pull the door from its frame.

He dashed down the stairs, but was late by only the fraction of a second, as a metal hand was just closing the huge door to the Graveyard of Genius. He fumbled at the secret combination, and as he was doing so Eva and Zita joined him.

The door swung open and they rushed through. But the place was deserted.

"They've carried your father through some secret passage," exclaimed Locke. "That would explain much that is strange that has happened about the house, too."

Just then Zita stepped forward with the plan in her hand. "See," she cried, "there is a secret passage marked on this."

Locke studied the plan for some time, but whoever had

drawn it had carefully concealed both the exact location of the passage and the method by which it was reached. As he searched, however, an idea occurred to Locke.

"I'll rig a trap with a camera," he decided, finally.

A few minutes later he returned to the room with his special quick-shutter camera, a flash-bag, and a ball of light twine. Carefully he focused the camera on the wall where the plan showed the secret passage to be. Then he rigged up the flash-bag and connected the whole with the twine, which he strung all about the Graveyard of Genius, so that, should any part of the wall move, it would cause the twine to break which in turn would at the same time release the shutter of the camera and explode the powder of the flashlight. Thus, without any direct human agency, a photograph would be taken.

Next he attached wires and ran them to the library above, where he installed an annunciator, the needle of which would indicate when the trap was sprung and the picture taken. Fascinated, the two girls watched. Eva was almost fainting with grief at the terrible fate that had overtaken her father. Even in his sickness, at least she had had him. But now he was gone—to what she could only guess. Locke tried to console her as they paced the library above, even though he realized that such consolation was hollow.

It was perhaps half an hour later when suddenly the needle of the annunciator began to vibrate rapidly. All leaped to their feet and ran down the stairs to the Graveyard.

At once Locke rushed to the camera, put in a slide, and took out the plate-holder. Then they hurried up to his laboratory.

There Locke procured a developing-bag and started to work. Nervously and impatiently Eva and Zita watched him at

Arthur B. Reeve and John W. Grey

his task.

At last the negative was ready and Locke drew it from the bag and held it to the light.

There, glaring out of the plate, was the devilish face of Balcom!

Eva and Zita both uttered a cry of astonishment and consternation. Even Locke was amazed. But the strongest feeling he had was anger as he turned to them.

"You two take this plan," he exclaimed. "It shows a den with an exit indicated. Get some one to go with you; find the place and wait for me there. I can find the secret entrance from the Graveyard from this negative—and I'm going through it."

Balcom, in the passageway between the Graveyard of Genius and the Automaton's den, was livid with fury. He realized that his picture had been taken, surmised that the secret passage would be found and that some assault on the den would be attempted. But he had had no time to locate the camera, which Locke had hidden well, nor had he dared to search longer for it when he heard Locke bounding down the stairs from the library.

Accordingly, he had retreated and hastened back through the passageway into the Automaton's den.

"Quick!" he shouted to the horde of emissaries in the place. "Bring dynamite, electric wires, and a rack-bar. They think they have us trapped. But if they try to follow me here, I tell you it will mean certain death to them."

The emissaires hastened to obey him. They brought the explosive and the means to detonate it, and carried the stuff into the passageway, where they made the connections. An emissary stepped forward and volunteered to use the rack-bar when the time came, but Balcom waved him away.

"No," he growled. "No one can take my revenge from me. I'll do the killing."

The emissaries fell back and went into the den.

Balcom was making some final adjustments when the great rock separating the passageway from the Graveyard of Genius swung slowly on its balanced hinges.

Startled from his work, even though he had expected the thing, Balcom looked up, and in the passageway caught a glimpse of the dim outline of his arch-enemy, Locke.

Balcom had been right. Locke had found the clue to the secret entrance to the tunnel.

He worked feverishly to complete the final connection, but almost before he finished Locke charged and the battle was on.

Up and down the passageway they fought. Although Locke was the younger man, yet in Balcom he found a giant of strength.

It was a fight between these two alone, for no emissary, no Automaton, now entered that passage of death.

Neither uttered a sound. Neither had a weapon. It was the primitive struggle of man to man for life.

But now Locke's youth and clean living began to tell in his favor and he sensed that his adversary was weakening. He redoubled his efforts.

After a particularly vicious blow from Locke, Balcom threw up his hands and toppled over backward—in the direction of the rack-bar itself.

Locke tried to throw Balcom's body out of the way. It was too late. With a thud Balcom crashed full upon the plunger, driving it home.

There was a blinding flash, a dull roar, and the earth rocked. Huge boulders were tossed about like feathers and the roof of the passage caved in.

Balcom was killed instantly. Locke, with better fortune, had been hurled to the ground, where the earth and rocks, in falling, had formed a sort of arch over his body.

He was alive, though barely conscious. He knew that soon a search would be made for him. But, buried under tons of earth and rock, could any rescuers reach him in time? Was this the end?

CHAPTER XXIV

For a long time Locke lay quite still. The shock to his nervous system had been terrific, and, although physically almost uninjured, he had lost his usual grip on himself and felt very helpless.

He felt terribly tired. The thought came to him that he had done enough, reached his limit of endurance. He craved sleep, a long sleep, and forgetfulness.

But youth and the undying desire for life and accomplishment won over this deadly mood and he began to take note of his position. His mind became clearer and the ringing in his ears, caused by the explosion, gradually passed away.

Then, like a flash, the question entered his mind of how he was able, buried under tons of debris, to breathe so freely. Why was the air not vitiated?

He tried to move slowly and quietly so as not to dislodge any of the rocks that formed an arch over his body. He succeeded beyond his expectations, for his body was in a sort of natural pocket and not one of his limbs was inextricably bound. Thus, twisting his body, he managed to draw himself into what seemed to be an even more open space.

Arthur B. Reeve and John W. Grey

He hardly dared to breathe, so fearful was he that any moment he might reach a point where further progress would be impossible. He moved slowly, gropingly, then suddenly he recoiled in horror, for his hand had come in contact with something which he recognized to be a man's face.

In his shaken condition it was some seconds before he could control the wild jangling of his nerves. Then he searched his pockets and, finding a match, lighted it. There, covered to the armpits by dirt and rocks, was the body of Balcom, whose last act before his own death had been an attempt to murder Locke.

Locke shuddered and redoubled his efforts to escape from the gruesome place. There still remained a small hole through which he must climb. But he negotiated it successfully, and in another moment he was aboveground and free.

Eva and Zita had followed Locke's instructions, but had not waited to find any one to go with them to the exit from the den. Nor did they wait at the exit more than a few minutes.

Eva had taken a small electric torch with her, and, becoming impatient at the non-appearance of Locke, she flashed it about as she followed the lines and marks indicated on the plan of the den.

She and Zita were surprised at the magnitude of the entrance passageway they uncovered. They had had to make a detour in order to reach the beach at a point where it was indicated that the exit of the den would be found, and even with the plan, which they consulted at every step, they almost missed their objective, for the cleft in the rocks slanted inward and was difficult to see even when one was standing directly in front of it.

They had peered into the cavern and were waiting when they heard the explosion. They gazed at each other questioningly and with apprehension.

"What do you think it is?" asked Eva, questioningly.

Zita could, of course, offer no explanation and did not try.

Impulsively both girls took a very foolish chance. Both had thought of Locke and they started to run into the cave entrance and toward the sound of the explosion.

Zita was in the lead, and it was at this moment that the panic-stricken emissaries came tumbling and fighting their way from the den. Zita shrieked to Eva to save herself, and Eva, although unwilling to leave her, knew that now she could do nothing to save Zita, and took her only chance of escape.

As for Zita, the emissaries were too frightened to pay any attention to her. But behind them came the iron monster, without nerves, it seemed. The Automaton saw her and pinned her to the rock wall until she was unconscious. Then, picking her up as though she were a feather, it carried her out to the beach.

Locke, the moment he freed himself from the hole which had so nearly been his grave, ran staggering toward the beach, for he felt instinctively that Eva and Zita were in danger.

Eva and Locke must have started at about the same time, she in her flight away from the Automaton, and Locke to find the den exit, for they met on the cliffside.

"Thank God you are safe!" exclaimed Eva.

Locke impulsively threw his arms about her and kissed her as they related their narrow escapes.

Locke resolved to follow the trail of the Automaton and to rescue Zita. Also he had hopes of rescuing Eva's father at the same time. Eva wished to accompany him, but he would not think of it, and insisted that she return to Brent Rock and keep all the doors barricaded. In fact, he followed her almost to the house and saw that she entered safely, then hurried back to the beach.

With the aid of Eva's electric torch, which she had given him, it was no difficult task to trace the huge footsteps of the Automaton, though, one by one, the footprints of the emissaries took divergent directions, probably for the very purpose of confusing just such a pursuit.

He followed the main track, however, until he came to the banks of a small stream, and there the trail was completely lost, for the monster had stepped into the water. Locke waded to the other bank and hunted for further tracks, but there were none to be found. The Automaton had undoubtedly waded up-stream to the point where he had decided to dispose of Zita.

Nothing daunted, Locke started wading upstream. This stream ran in a gully between the rocks and the cliffs on either side, which were very high. Time and time again Locke thought of turning back for more searchers. But he hated to return to Eva without at least some news, and therefore he persisted.

He was at last rewarded, for just as he was about to turn to the right where the stream made a bend, he thought he heard a low laugh. He stopped dead in his tracks. Again the sound of the broken laughter came to him.

Cautiously Locke moved slowly forward until he could see around the bend.

It was a strange sight that met his gaze. Under an enormous overhanging rock he saw about fifteen men standing, while against the cliff he could distinguish the form of a girl. It was undoubtedly Zita. Sitting on a rock and quite close to her was Peter Brent.

The emissaries were clustered around the central figure, which was waving its arms of steel and indicating what they should do. As the Automaton gesticulated, tiny points of fire gleamed from its eyes.

Seen in the light of the lanterns held by the emissaries, the Automaton never looked more terrifying. Even Locke himself, who had encountered the monster so often, felt a cold chill as he watched him and his men.

Locke turned noiselessly, for well he knew that alone he could do nothing. He started to retrace his steps to Brent Rock, and no sooner had he arrived there than he told Eva that her father still lived and was uninjured, and that Zita was safe in the new den of the Automaton which he had discovered. Then he telephoned to his chief to send officers immediately to Brent Rock.

After the explosion that had killed Balcom and had come so near to killing Locke, when he had finally rescued himself and had drawn himself out of the hole, there was one who watched him.

It was none other than that mysterious being, Doctor Q. What twist of that disordered brain had brought him to the spot was not at once evident. However, as soon as Locke had left to go toward Eva, Doctor Q came from his hiding-place, madly smiling and wagging his head. He peered into

Arthur B. Reeve and John W. Grey

the hole and, seeing nothing, lighted a match and thrust it far down into the darkness.

There was a sharp intake of his breath, for the match revealed to him the dead face of Herbert Balcom.

Doctor Q drew back and stood erect.

"Dead!" he muttered, as he ran his fingers through his hair dazedly.

"Dead!"

A strange thing happened. The mad light fled from the eyes of Doctor Q and the twisted brain seemed to become clear.

Suddenly in the very field the old man knelt down and prayed a thankful prayer for his recovery.

What was the strange power which Balcom had wielded over him, which death had snapped?

The officers arrived at Brent Rock and Locke was ready. The party left immediately to go to the rescue of Brent and Zita, and it took them only a short time to reach the spot which Locke had located.

Disposing some of his force below the hanging rock, Locke and some others went farther upstream. The two parties looked at their watches, waiting a certain time agreed on.

Then the two parties moved toward each other. As they came in sight of the spot, Locke experienced a keen disappointment. He could see no one. Advancing farther, he discovered Brent still on the same rock. Guarding him were three emissaries. That was all. Zita, the Automaton, and the other emissaries were gone.

The three emissaries, seeing the numbers opposed to them, did not even offer to resist. They were placed under arrest, but nothing could induce them to tell where the others had gone.

To fail Zita after she had so nobly saved his life in the lair of the hypnotist was an unwelcome thought to Locke, and he resolved to rescue her at any risk. But first he felt he must restore Brent to his daughter, and therefore the party returned to Brent Rock.

Eva was beside herself with joy at the safe return of her father, and led him tenderly to his room and sent immediately for the doctor in order that he might not suffer from his exposure.

While this was going on at Brent Rock, Paul Balcom was rifling his father's papers in the apartment where Balcom had lived. He had unceremoniously thrown letters and documents all over the floor in his mad search for something. Finally he found what he was looking for, and, smiling triumphantly as he read the paper, he thrust it into his pocket and hurriedly left the place, not stopping even to pick up the papers scattered all about.

Zita had evidently been watching the house, for no sooner had he left than she ran up the front steps of the Balcom apartment.

In some way she had procured a key and let herself in. Then began a feverish search very similar to that which Paul had instituted. Only, this time Zita picked up all the papers, arranging them and placing them back in the drawers, after scanning their contents.

She had almost finished when a small book lying in a distant corner of the room caught her eye.

At a glance she saw that it was a diary. Turning the pages rapidly, she finally came to one over which she fairly gloated, for its information, sold to the proper parties, might make her independent for life.

Even as she was gloating over her find there came the sound of many feet in the front hallway. Zita had no time to run out of the room before the door opened, giving entrance to six emissaries, surrounding her.

The emissaries locked all the doors and tramped out. Only their leader remained for a moment to throw a parting shot.

"Remember," he threatened, "this house is watched. See that you act accordingly. You will, if you know what's good for you."

Then he slammed the door and locked it behind him.

For a long time Zita sat there, too despairing to move. Then her ear caught the sound of stealthy footsteps in the hall, and she ran and hid behind the portieres. The door opened slowly and Paul stole again into the room.

Having nothing to fear from him, Zita came from her hiding-place and confronted him. Paul was startled for a moment at her sudden appearance, but recovered himself on seeing that it was Zita.

The paper that he had stolen from his father's desk had proved to him that Zita had become highly desirable, and he was not one to miss such an opportunity.

As he questioned her, Zita told him briefly her story, or, rather, such portions of it as she thought it desirable for him to know. Paul, in turn, assured her of his undying friendship and something more. His earnestness almost made it seem true, and he talked in his most fascinating and attractive manner. He finally ended his conversation with a direct proposal of marriage. But he had overstepped the mark and Zita was not to be fooled.

"Paul"—she laughed scornfully now—"you should be on the stage. It needed only this proposal to prove to me that I am really Peter Brent's daughter."

"Peter Brent's daughter!" he exclaimed. "No, not his daughter—the daughter of Doctor Q."

"Impossible!" recoiled Zita, astounded at the assertion.

"True, Zita," he asserted, "absolutely true. Here, look at this paper."

With hands that trembled, Zita took the paper and read an amazing table. Unless the paper lied, she was indeed the daughter of Doctor Q.

There was only one thing to do and that was to confront Doctor Q at once and force him to a full explanation.

In order not to antagonize Paul, Zita was now particularly nice to him. Her object was to get him to consent to her escape, so that she could inform Locke and Eva of her discovery and all three confront Doctor Q and wrest from him the story.

At first Paul would not let her go unless she consented to marry him, but Zita played him skilfully, so that finally he unlocked the door.

Then Zita flew down the stairs and to a telephone around the corner, where she called up Locke, to whom she told as much as she dared over the wire.

Locke told her that he and Eva would meet her within an hour in the lobby of one of the city's largest hotels, and Zita hastened there, where she waited impatiently until they arrived.

Doctor Q admitted them immediately, and they noticed with astonishment the wonderful change for the better that had taken place in the man. For with the restoration of his mind all the evil lines of his face had been obliterated, as it were, and in the place of the doddering half-imbecile they found a genial, kindly, and distinguished gentleman who, with the utmost hospitality, brought chairs and begged them to be seated.

Zita, in her anxiety to know the truth, could hardly contain her impatience. Tossed from pillar to post, dominated once by the strong, evil mind of Balcom, Zita had run the gamut of human emotions before she had barely passed her girlhood.

Seeing her agitation, Locke undertook to interrogate the doctor.

"Doctor Q," he began, "I believe you know the perpetrator of the crimes to which we have all been subjected, and we have come to you in all friendliness to ask you to clear this mystery up for us. Balcom is dead," added Locke, pointedly.

"Yes, I know that," interrupted Doctor Q.

"You know?" all asked. "How do you know?"

The doctor told of having seen Balcom's body. But at first he could not explain why he was in the spot at the time.

Then Locke went on to tell him of the document that Paul had shown to Zita.

Doctor Q sank heavily into a chair.

"That document that Paul Balcom showed Zita," he exclaimed, after a moment, "told the truth."

All were startled. Zita would have risen with a cry had not Locke gently touched her arm.

"Tell us the story," demanded Locke of Q.

For some moments Doctor Q seemed to be collecting his scattered thoughts, as though still a haze hung over his mind. Then he began to speak, becoming more certain of his strange story.

"It was many years ago," he began, as all drew closer about him, listening breathlessly to his narrative, "and all these years I have been quite mad. The man now lying dead, Balcom, was the cause of all these years of misery."

The old man passed his hand over his head as though to wipe away a recollection of hate and fear, then resumed:

"I was an inventor in those days, and very successful. I had built up a great fortune, had built a great house, and in that house I had a beautiful wife and two of the loveliest children, a boy and a girl, that ever man had."

He paused again, then went on:

"One day, a man entered my life and proposed to put my inventions on the market very advantageously. He was suave, polished, and apparently a gentleman. At any rate, I trusted him. You all knew him. It was Herbert Balcom.

"At the time I did not know that in order to give my inventions a clear field the inventions of hundreds of poor

Arthur B. Reeve and John W. Grey

inventors were to be suppressed. I know now, Miss Brent, that your own father was led along in the scheme, even as I was. Balcom possessed the master mind and we were all as children in his hands."

Doctor Q stopped a moment. It was evident that he was speaking with restraint when it came to Peter Brent, perhaps glossing over what the man had done. Though he did not say so, the mere fact that at last Brent had seen the light and had planned a wholesale restitution weighed supremely in Doctor Q's mind.

"One day," he resumed, "Balcom came to me in what I know now was merely feigned excitement and fear. 'They're after us!' he cried. 'Brent and I have done our best—but the government is after you, and we can't protect you any longer.'"

"Then for the first time Balcom told me of the real purposes of the company, told me that he had been drawn into it by Brent. It was all a tissue of lies—lies that drove me from my home and country. I hated your father with an undying hate, Miss Brent.

"Well, to make the sad story short, I took my wife and children and sailed secretly for the farthermost parts of the world. Off the coast of Madagascar, in the Straits, a typhoon came up. The vessel was driven on the rocks and wrecked. I was cast ashore, and I vaguely remember how, for days and weeks, I patrolled that beach, subsisting on shell-fish, imploring God, day and night, to restore my wife and children to me. Then my mind gave way.

"The natives took me in, thinking me a god. They took me many miles inland. Savages, the world over, are superstitious about the demented, and so they treated me kindly. They installed me in a thatched hut of my own and made me a leader.

"How many months, years, I stayed with them I do not know. But, true to my mechanical instinct, I rigged up a forge and improved many of the crude instruments of the natives, principally those of agriculture.

"But transcending every other feeling, I hated Brent. In my madness, I conceived the idea that I would construct an iron giant that, upon its completion, if I could only procure the brain of a man who had died of a lightning stroke or other electric agency, I could, by installing this brain in the brain cavity of the giant, give it volition, make it a superman without feeling or conscience. It was a mad idea—but I was mad.

"At about this time Balcom came to Madagascar. He found me and, knowing my intense hatred of Peter Brent, he cruelly added fuel to the fire. Already he must have known that Brent was coming to his senses and planning his great restitution to genius.

"He promised me that if I would come to New York with him he would secure an electrocuted brain so that I could perfect my steel automaton and obtain my revenge. I was easily persuaded and I sailed with Balcom, bringing the iron monster with me."

A strange light gleamed in the old man's eyes as he spoke, not the light of madness, but of kindliness now.

"Children," he said, at length, "I have, during these lucid moments, watched you all closely. Call it instinct if you will, but you, Zita, and you, Quentin, seem to be particularly dear to me now. To-day, returning from the scene of the explosion, with every faculty not only clear, but rather sharpened by long disuse, I pieced the years, the months, even the days together. I searched in an old trunk and I found—this."

It was a list of those rescued from the steamer *Magnifique*, and with amazement they read the names among the passengers:

QUENTIN LOCKE
ZITA LOCKE

There was a short note at the bottom of the list, to the effect that no trace of either the father or the mother of the two children had been found.

Paper after paper which Doctor Q had found, where they had been preserved by Balcom, proved the identification and the story.

Locke's head was in a whirl at the sudden change in relationships, but not more so than Zita's. Finally Zita could stand the strain no longer. What had been a hopeless love was now explained.

"My—my brother!" she sobbed, as she buried her head on Quentin's shoulder.

Both turned to Doctor Q—Doctor Q no longer, but really Quentin Locke, senior, whence had come the "Q."

His eyes filled with tears and his voice choked.

"My—children," he murmured, "I see that it is not too late for me to find happiness, after all. Our enemy is dead. It was Balcom, of course, who was in that frame of armor, who used that terrible poison that stole away Brent's mind. The iron monster will walk no more. Henceforth Peter Brent and Miss Eva and you, Quentin—will—"

Doctor Q had not time to finish the sentence.

The door burst inward.

The Automaton, its eyes aflame, stalked in among them!

CHAPTER XXV

As the Automaton crashed its way into the room all sprang back terrified, aghast.

For this monster, they had felt sure, was now nothing but an inanimate shell of armor, since Balcom was dead.

Yet here it was, stalking toward them and evidently as bent on destruction as ever.

What did it mean?

In an instant Locke had helped Eva through an open window and turned to assist Zita. But Doctor Q forestalled him and had already taken her in his arms and had fled with her into another room.

For the moment Locke was surprised to see that the Automaton totally ignored him. Instead, it stalked to the door and wrenched it open. There, cowering in the hall, in abject terror, was De Luxe Dora.

How and why she had come there was a mystery. But the Automaton did not hesitate. It raised its hands and, as it did so, long flashes of blue flame leaped from the steel finger-tips toward the unfortunate woman. Once she shrieked, then crumpled and fell dead.

The monster then turned its attention to Locke, striding toward him with a menacing gesture. But the diversion due to Dora had given all just the time they needed to make good their flight. Locke threw a chair to impede the progress of the monster, and then, as he saw that all the others were safe, he lightly vaulted out of the window himself, to find them waiting for him in the little yard below.

"What do you make of it now—father?" asked Locke of Doctor Q. "Balcom is dead. Who is now in the iron man?"

Doctor Q shrugged. It was a mystery to him as much as ever, and he seemed unable to throw any light on it.

"But De Luxe Dora," queried Zita. "What had she come for? Why was she struck down—first?"

Again Doctor Q shook his head.

From the yard they could hear the Automaton's heavy tread in the room and, as there was nothing to be gained by remaining, they left the yard and hurried away out of the neighborhood.

They had not gone far, however, when Doctor Locke came to a full stop.

"I must go back," he exclaimed.

For a moment all thought he had again taken leave of his senses. Yet he was obdurate.

"Miss Brent—Eva," he explained, "you know that a grievous wrong has been done your father through me. He lies ill of that most terrible of diseases, the laughing madness. I alone possess the antidote, and it is in the laboratory that we have just left. I pray that that iron beast

Arthur B. Reeve and John W. Grey

has not destroyed it."

At the mere words Locke turned as if to go back for it.

"No, Quentin," remonstrated his father. "You must remain to guard Eva."

"Then I will go," insisted Zita. "I am not afraid now. Even when the monster carried me off I overcame my fear, watched my chance, and escaped from his den, where he left me. I will go."

Finally Doctor Locke agreed that Zita might return with him, remain outside, and give the alarm if anything happened to him. Thus, after many remonstrances, it was agreed, and Eva and Quentin went on to Brent Rock.

No one had molested Brent in the mean time. The terror caused by the explosion, as well as the loss of Balcom, for the time, at least, had evidently cowed the emissary band.

While Eva made Brent comfortable, Locke went immediately to the laboratory, where he had something which he considered very important.

"Quentin," remarked Eva, as she joined him, "your father spoke the truth, I believe, when he said that it was Balcom in the Automaton, But if that was the case, who is in it now?"

Locke shook his head dubiously. "I give it up," he replied. "It's too deep for me. But whoever it is, he won't trouble us long, I'll wager. I've been perfecting a special gun and an explosive-gas bullet. No one can shoot the monster. Nothing seems to stop it. But this weapon, I think, will at last prove a match for it."

Eva, who had always had the deepest interest in Quentin's work, listened attentively as he explained in detail the working of the new weapon.

"And now we come to the actual loading of these asphyxiating-poison bullets," concluded Quentin. "I really must ask you, Eva, to go into another room, for it is dangerous work and you must not risk your life here."

"But, Quentin," remonstrated Eva, "we've risked our lives so often together that I have ceased to be afraid of anything."

Quentin was insistent, and finally Eva agreed.

As Doctor Q and Zita neared the former's laboratory, they saw that all the lights in the house were out. Doctor Locke, against Zita's advice, insisted on going in, and told his daughter to wait outside. It was then that Zita disobeyed her father for the first time, for she flatly refused to be left behind.

"No," she insisted. "I found a father to-night and what we must risk we risk together. It is no worse than the peril from which I once escaped."

There was no reasoning with Zita, and they let themselves into the little yard and went up the back steps. When they came to the door of the laboratory they listened intently.

There was no sound. Then they mustered up courage and cautiously entered the room. For a long time they stood quite still, not daring to move. Finally Doctor Q suddenly lighted a match.

The room was in terrible confusion, as though cyclone-swept.

Arthur B. Reeve and John W. Grey

Doctor Locke turned on an electric bulb and the room was flooded with light.

Everywhere there were traces of the Automaton. But the monster itself had left the place. Doctor Locke crossed to the other door. There was a sight that made them shudder. The body of De Luxe Dora was still huddled in a heap on the floor. She was quite dead.

But Doctor Locke had no time now to waste. Moments were precious. At any instant they might again be attacked. Feverishly he began to search for the bottle containing the antidote.

At last he found it, carefully hidden, and in a bottle fortunately not broken.

They left everything as it was and hurriedly left the place, on their way to Brent Rock.

Meanwhile, in one of the worst quarters of the city, down in the cellar of a huge warehouse, a mob of emissaries were gathered. They were discussing the things that had led up to the explosion in the Automaton's den, Balcom's death, and the arrest of their three pals. Plans for the future they discussed, but, with their leader gone, these hardened men were still as helpless as children.

Suddenly above the din of voices a strange, familiar sound was heard, a sound as of clanking chains, and the blood froze in the veins of every man present. Then with wild shouts of terror they scattered in every direction, for the Automaton was stalking toward them.

Balcom, the man who had given the iron man life, was dead. And yet the Automaton was among them!

That night, in the holds of many vessels and on the brake-beams of many trains pulling away from the city, emissaries who once were slaves of the Automaton were fleeing the city in every direction.

When Zita and her father arrived at Brent Rock, Locke was still working at his new gas-gun. Eva was in the library, but when she heard the voices in the hallway she ran to welcome them.

"Oh, I'm so glad you've both returned safe," she cried. Then, unable to withstand the suspense longer, she asked, "Have you brought it—the antidote?"

When Doctor Locke told her that the bottle that contained it was safely stowed in his pocket Eva sank, overwrought, into a chair and cried with simple relief and joy.

In a moment, however, she had gained control of herself, dashed the tears from her eyes, and almost seized the bottle from Doctor Locke.

"Bring him down here, my dear," cautioned the doctor, still holding the bottle. "You would not know how to administer it."

Eva ran to her father's room, stopping only long enough to summon Quentin, then together they led Brent down-stairs.

Brent's condition was still pitiable. His mind was a total blank. These people—Doctor Q, Zita, Quentin, even his own daughter—meant nothing to him. He lived and breathed. But no ray of light entered the poor brain.

They guided his halting steps into the library as if he had been something less than a child, and placed him in the same big armchair on which he had sunk the fatal morning that the fumes from the candles had overcome him.

Doctor Q drew out the bottle and, telling Zita to bring a glass of water, measured out a few drops of the antidote, pouring them into the glass. Then he moved over to Brent and tried to get him to drink it. For a long time Brent merely clenched his teeth, but, once he was induced to taste the mixture, he drank it eagerly.

For ages, it seemed to those watching, Brent sat as before, vacantly gazing straight ahead of him—so long, in fact, that a terrible fear entered Eva's heart that, perhaps, after all, the antidote would fail and that her father would remain without reason until the day of his death.

Then slowly a change was noticeable in his eyes, and all leaned forward with overpowering intentness. What they were watching was like a miracle. Slowly, very slowly, they saw the soul creep back into those poor, mad eyes.

Brent had been staring directly at his daughter as she watched him anxiously. Now a puzzled look came over his face and, raising a hand, he rubbed his forehead.

Then a wonderful light seemed to shine from his eyes and he held out his arms to Eva.

With a sob of excited happiness Eva rushed to embrace him.

As Locke stood behind him, Zita and Doctor Q walked to the other end of the room, turning sidewise to the group.

Suddenly Brent turned his eyes away from Eva and noticed Doctor Q for the first time.

"Who is that?" he asked Eva.

"Why, father, that is—"

At the sound of voices Doctor Q had turned around.

"You!" gasped Brent, as he sank back into his chair.

The look on his face was strange, perhaps half fear, half shame.

Doctor Q came no nearer for a moment, while Eva hastened to explain what had happened. Then unsteadily Brent rose and walked over to the doctor.

"You are alive!" he exclaimed. "You have come again into my life so that at last I can make restitution. My daughter has explained to me all that you have suffered. Believe me it was through my own weakness. It seems incredible that any man could be so infamous, so utterly without moral scruples, as was Balcom. I believed the villain implicitly. That is, and can be, my only excuse."

The doctor placed his hand on Brent's shoulder.

"I can understand only too well," he remarked, "for I, too, believed in Balcom. You were a reticent man and so my dealings were all with him. I was gullible, an inventor, not a business man. I should have come to you before I fled the country, I suppose. Say no more about it, for I forgive you from the bottom of my heart."

But Brent insisted on explaining that at least he had had a desire to right the great wrongs.

"I can remember it all now," he continued. "I was about to make restitution when a man connected with the company —I am sure now that he was an adventurer, a crook, in the pay of Balcom, although Balcom probably tried to hide it—

Arthur B. Reeve and John W. Grey

came to me. His name, as I remember it, was Flint. I was about to write a letter that showed that it was my intention to right a wrong, when—something interrupted me and—the rest I can't remember."

Quentin, who had been standing behind the chair, now drew from his pocket a piece of paper which he handed to Brent.

"Yes—that is it," cried Brent, excitedly, taking it, and spreading it out before them. "See!"

It was a note addressed to Quentin Locke and read:

I have done you a great wrong about which you know nothing, but for which I will make amends—

"It was broken off," exclaimed Brent, making a sad effort to recollect what had happened. "I don't remember how. But this Flint had been telling me something about an iron monster. He had a model—said he had seen the real thing in Madagascar, that it had a human brain, that it walked and fought, that it had strength and life—but no conscience. He hinted that the thing would do me harm if I persisted in a course that I had determined for myself of giving back to inventors we had robbed the things of which we had robbed them. I did not believe him. I thought the thing absurd, and started to write the note, going a step farther than I had ever threatened Balcom."

Quentin, Doctor Q, and Zita exchanged glances as Eva's father resumed his narrative.

"Then I felt a choking sensation at my throat. I remember the effrontery of Flint's laughing at me, in a maudlin sort of way, and then—a blank. The next I recall was just now—Eva gazing at me with a worried expression in her dear eyes.

I called to her and kissed her, tried to comfort her. Then I saw you, Locke, and Zita."

Peter Brent, from the time he and Flint had been overcome by the fumes from the candelabra until he received the antidote and recognized his daughter, had not known a thing!

As they talked there were many matters the two aged men discovered while they pieced together the happenings of years.

Each had been duped by the same man. Each had suffered great trouble through this man's machinations and duplicity.

As they talked, the attention of both turned to the younger Quentin Locke, who seemed overjoyed at the recovery of his former employer.

Brent had a very great feeling of affection and respect for the younger man, for had he not really brought him up?

As all questioned one another, they asked Brent much about the past, and he told them all.

He told how he had become finally suspicious of Balcom, of how he insisted upon instituting a search for the doctor, his wife, and children. He told how Balcom had opposed him up to the last moment. Then he described his sailing half the world over in search of them, how at times he found a trail, only to lose it again.

Finally he told how at last he had found that the mother had been lost, but the children saved.

"I was in Bombay," he continued, "in despair that I would

ever find any of you. At that time I was an old man before my time, for my conscience gave me no rest. I went down to the quay to purchase a ticket for my return to New York, and, true to the habit I had formed, I asked the ticket-seller if he had ever heard anything of the survivors of the steamer *Magnifique*.

"'Do I know anything of it?' repeated the ticket-seller. 'No, but there's a man working on this dock now who never talks of anything else. He was a sailor on the ship and one of the few who survived.'"

"You can believe me when I tell you that I ran down that dock and found the man. He remembered you all well, remembered you children when you were taken up with some other survivors, and he said he thought that some family had taken you to Hong-Kong.

"I canceled my passage to Liverpool and immediately sailed for China. Still, my troubles were not over, for it was weeks before I finally located you babies, Quentin and Zita.

"I won't burden you with the difficulties I encountered before the English family, the Danes, with whom I found you, would consent to give you up. Nor will I take time to tell of our return to New York through San Francisco.

"Let it suffice for you to know that we arrived safely after I had completely circled the world. I sent you to good schools, and when Zita was old enough I made her my secretary so that I could watch over her. Quentin, being older, I had not dared to have around at first. I feared he might question me too closely. And what answer could I give him? Could I tell him that International Patents had driven his father into exile, that I had been partly the cause, the indirect cause, it is true, but still the cause of his mother's death? I never found the courage to do that and so

I sent him to a preparatory school and later to college. Years wiped out his childhood recollections and when he came here he came as a stranger employed in the company's laboratory. I make no defense, but I assure you all that my own sufferings have atoned for all the wrongs I have done."

Brent broke down and was almost weeping, when Quentin and Eva moved over to his side and reassured him.

As soon as Brent had recovered from his weakness he wanted to know all that had happened since he had been unconscious under the drug, and as he listened he was aghast at the Automaton and Balcom's villainy.

"I've something here that will stop him, though," added Quentin, as he showed the new gas-gun he had invented and explained its deadly properties. "Bring him on again— I'm ready."

"Quentin—please don't joke about that terrible monster," shivered Eva. "It has injured us so often—I don't even want to talk about it—or about the government that asked you to come here and set things right. Let us forget—now that all is right."

Quentin smiled at her and his quick mind saw that the time had come to guide the conversation into pleasanter channels. He moved close to Brent.

"It looks, Mr. Brent," he said, quietly, "as though we all were at about the end of our troubles. But there are two of us here who are not quite happy—yet. Mr. Brent, I am going to claim a reward."

"Anything, my dear Locke, anything I have is yours."

"Then I may as well tell you that Eva and I love each other

and I want your consent to our marriage."

Brent beamed.

"That, Quentin, is the dearest wish my heart can have."

Quentin turned to Eva to take her in his arms when there was a terrific crash of glass in the conservatory, the splintering of wood, and the Automaton, arms swinging like flails, charged like a mad thing into the room.

Its terrorizing eyes were agleam, its one desire destruction. A large table stood in its way and it demolished it as though it were matchwood.

The interruption came so abruptly that Brent, who in his right mind had never seen the fiend and was now seeing it for the first time, was paralyzed with horror. He tried to rise from his chair, but in his weak condition fell back, helpless.

Quentin made a flying leap over the demolished table and placed himself directly in front of Brent and in the path of the monster. Doctor Q, Zita, and Eva started for Locke's side, but he waved them back frantically.

Locke reached into his pocket and drew out his gas-pistol. The Automaton was almost upon him when he raised his arm and fired.

There was a blinding flash and a dull report. The Automaton stopped in his tracks and, raising one mighty hand to its chest, staggered backward. Again Quentin fired, and the Automaton slowly crumpled, sinking to one knee. There was no need to fire again, for suddenly the monster crashed to the floor and lay still.

Locke started forward, but Eva shrieked for him to stand

back. She had not forgotten that once she had thought the monster dead and it had suddenly seized her and almost crushed out her life.

There was, however, nothing to fear this time. Quentin reassured her that the gas fumes had passed away, then knelt by the iron terror. He tried to remove the steel headpiece, but before he could accomplish it the doctor came forward and in a moment had unfastened the bolts.

As they were doing so a thick voice from inside could be distinguished, muttering words about the capture of Brent and Zita just before Balcom was killed, the escape of Zita, the rescue of Brent, the killing of Dora, who had evidently come to betray something in jealousy. It was all incoherent and Doctor Q and Quentin hastened to uncasque the man within.

They lifted off the helmet and there was the contorted and dying face of Paul Balcom, who had, in desperation, taken his father's place in a vain hope to secure the fortune for himself.

The poison was too strong, and as the girls turned, sickened, away, the evil features froze, more evil than ever they had been in his evil life.

* * * * *

A few days later a brilliant wedding took place at Brent Rock, which itself was a present to the bride and groom.

After the guests had thinned out, Quentin and Eva strolled into the garden, no longer in fear of attack from the steel Automaton.

Eva glanced at her ring, musing.

Arthur B. Reeve and John W. Grey

"After all the things from which you have escaped, dear," she murmured, a bit timidly, "I am afraid nothing in the world can hold you."

Quentin drew her into his arms, while her hand rested on his shoulder, and kissed the little golden ring that encircled her finger.

"Nothing but that band of love," he smiled.

Choose from Thousands of 1stWorldLibrary Classics By

A. M. Barnard	Booth Tarkington	Edward Everett Hale
Ada Leverson	Boyd Cable	Edward J. O'Biren
Adolphus William Ward	Bram Stoker	Edward S. Ellis
Aesop	C. Collodi	Edwin L. Arnold
Agatha Christie	C. E. Orr	Eleanor Atkins
Alexander Aaronsohn	C. M. Ingleby	Eleanor Hallowell Abbott
Alexander Kielland	Carolyn Wells	Eliot Gregory
Alexandre Dumas	Catherine Parr Traill	Elizabeth Gaskell
Alfred Gatty	Charles A. Eastman	Elizabeth McCracken
Alfred Ollivant	Charles Amory Beach	Elizabeth Von Arnim
Alice Duer Miller	Charles Dickens	Ellem Key
Alice Turner Curtis	Charles Dudley Warner	Emerson Hough
Alice Dunbar	Charles Farrar Browne	Emilie F. Carlen
Allen Chapman	Charles Ives	Emily Bronte
Alleyne Ireland	Charles Kingsley	Emily Dickinson
Ambrose Bierce	Charles Klein	Enid Bagnold
Amelia E. Barr	Charles Hanson Towne	Enilor Macartney Lane
Amory H. Bradford	Charles Lathrop Pack	Erasmus W. Jones
Andrew Lang	Charles Romyn Dake	Ernie Howard Pie
Andrew McFarland Davis	Charles Whibley	Ethel May Dell
Andy Adams	Charles Willing Beale	Ethel Turner
Angela Brazil	Charlotte M. Braeme	Ethel Watts Mumford
Anna Alice Chapin	Charlotte M. Yonge	Eugene Sue
Anna Sewell	Charlotte Perkins Stetson	Eugenie Foa
Annie Besant	Clair W. Hayes	Eugene Wood
Annie Hamilton Donnell	Clarence Day Jr.	Eustace Hale Ball
Annie Payson Call	Clarence E. Mulford	Evelyn Everett-green
Annie Roe Carr	Clemence Housman	Everard Cotes
Annonaymous	Confucius	F. H. Cheley
Anton Chekhov	Coningsby Dawson	F. J. Cross
Archibald Lee Fletcher	Cornelis DeWitt Wilcox	F. Marion Crawford
Arnold Bennett	Cyril Burleigh	Fannie E. Newberry
Arthur C. Benson	D. H. Lawrence	Federick Austin Ogg
Arthur Conan Doyle	Daniel Defoe	Ferdinand Ossendowski
Arthur M. Winfield	David Garnett	Fergus Hume
Arthur Ransome	Dinah Craik	Florence A. Kilpatrick
Arthur Schnitzler	Don Carlos Janes	Fremont B. Deering
Arthur Train	Donald Keyhoe	Francis Bacon
Atticus	Dorothy Kilner	Francis Darwin
B.H. Baden-Powell	Dougan Clark	Frances Hodgson Burnett
B. M. Bower	Douglas Fairbanks	Frances Parkinson Keyes
B. C. Chatterjee	E. Nesbit	Frank Gee Patchin
Baroness Emmuska Orczy	E. P. Roe	Frank Harris
Baroness Orczy	E. Phillips Oppenheim	Frank Jewett Mather
Basil King	E. S. Brooks	Frank L. Packard
Bayard Taylor	Earl Barnes	Frank V. Webster
Ben Macomber	Edgar Rice Burroughs	Frederic Stewart Isham
Bertha Muzzy Bower	Edith Van Dyne	Frederick Trevor Hill
Bjornstjerne Bjornson	Edith Wharton	Frederick Winslow Taylor

Friedrich Kerst
Friedrich Nietzsche
Fyodor Dostoyevsky
G.A. Henty
G.K. Chesterton
Gabrielle E. Jackson
Garrett P. Serviss
Gaston Leroux
George A. Warren
George Ade
Geroge Bernard Shaw
George Cary Eggleston
George Durston
George Ebers
George Eliot
George Gissing
George MacDonald
George Meredith
George Orwell
George Sylvester Viereck
George Tucker
George W. Cable
George Wharton James
Gertrude Atherton
Gordon Casserly
Grace E. King
Grace Gallatin
Grace Greenwood
Grant Allen
Guillermo A. Sherwell
Gulielma Zollinger
Gustav Flaubert
H. A. Cody
H. B. Irving
H.C. Bailey
H. G. Wells
H. H. Munro
H. Irving Hancock
H. R. Naylor
H. Rider Haggard
H. W. C. Davis
Haldeman Julius
Hall Caine
Hamilton Wright Mabie
Hans Christian Andersen
Harold Avery
Harold McGrath
Harriet Beecher Stowe
Harry Castlemon
Harry Coghill
Harry Houidini

Hayden Carruth
Helent Hunt Jackson
Helen Nicolay
Hendrik Conscience
Hendy David Thoreau
Henri Barbusse
Henrik Ibsen
Henry Adams
Henry Ford
Henry Frost
Henry James
Henry Jones Ford
Henry Seton Merriman
Henry W Longfellow
Herbert A. Giles
Herbert Carter
Herbert N. Casson
Herman Hesse
Hildegard G. Frey
Homer
Honore De Balzac
Horace B. Day
Horace Walpole
Horatio Alger Jr.
Howard Pyle
Howard R. Garis
Hugh Lofting
Hugh Walpole
Humphry Ward
Ian Maclaren
Inez Haynes Gillmore
Irving Bacheller
Isabel Cecilia Williams
Isabel Hornibrook
Israel Abrahams
Ivan Turgenev
J.G.Austin
J. Henri Fabre
J. M. Barrie
J. M. Walsh
J. Macdonald Oxley
J. R. Miller
J. S. Fletcher
J. S. Knowles
J. Storer Clouston
J. W. Duffield
Jack London
Jacob Abbott
James Allen
James Andrews
James Baldwin

James Branch Cabell
James DeMille
James Joyce
James Lane Allen
James Lane Allen
James Oliver Curwood
James Oppenheim
James Otis
James R. Driscoll
Jane Abbott
Jane Austen
Jane L. Stewart
Janet Aldridge
Jens Peter Jacobsen
Jerome K. Jerome
Jessie Graham Flower
John Buchan
John Burroughs
John Cournos
John F. Kennedy
John Gay
John Glasworthy
John Habberton
John Joy Bell
John Kendrick Bangs
John Milton
John Philip Sousa
John Taintor Foote
Jonas Lauritz Idemil Lie
Jonathan Swift
Joseph A. Altsheler
Joseph Carey
Joseph Conrad
Joseph E. Badger Jr
Joseph Hergesheimer
Joseph Jacobs
Jules Vernes
Julian Hawthrone
Julie A Lippmann
Justin Huntly McCarthy
Kakuzo Okakura
Karle Wilson Baker
Kate Chopin
Kenneth Grahame
Kenneth McGaffey
Kate Langley Bosher
Kate Langley Bosher
Katherine Cecil Thurston
Katherine Stokes
L. A. Abbot
L. T. Meade

L. Frank Baum
Latta Griswold
Laura Dent Crane
Laura Lee Hope
Laurence Housman
Lawrence Beasley
Leo Tolstoy
Leonid Andreyev
Lewis Carroll
Lewis Sperry Chafer
Lilian Bell
Lloyd Osbourne
Louis Hughes
Louis Joseph Vance
Louis Tracy
Louisa May Alcott
Lucy Fitch Perkins
Lucy Maud Montgomery
Luther Benson
Lydia Miller Middleton
Lyndon Orr
M. Corvus
M. H. Adams
Margaret E. Sangster
Margret Howth
Margaret Vandercook
Margaret W. Hungerford
Margret Penrose
Maria Edgeworth
Maria Thompson Daviess
Mariano Azuela
Marion Polk Angellotti
Mark Overton
Mark Twain
Mary Austin
Mary Catherine Crowley
Mary Cole
Mary Hastings Bradley
Mary Roberts Rinehart
Mary Rowlandson
M. Wollstonecraft Shelley
Maud Lindsay
Max Beerbohm
Myra Kelly
Nathaniel Hawthrone
Nicolo Machiavelli
O. F. Walton
Oscar Wilde

Owen Johnson
P.G. Wodehouse
Paul and Mabel Thorne
Paul G. Tomlinson
Paul Severing
Percy Brebner
Percy Keese Fitzhugh
Peter B. Kyne
Plato
Quincy Allen
R. Derby Holmes
R. L. Stevenson
R. S. Ball
Rabindranath Tagore
Rahul Alvares
Ralph Bonehill
Ralph Henry Barbour
Ralph Victor
Ralph Waldo Emmerson
Rene Descartes
Ray Cummings
Rex Beach
Rex E. Beach
Richard Harding Davis
Richard Jefferies
Richard Le Gallienne
Robert Barr
Robert Frost
Robert Gordon Anderson
Robert L. Drake
Robert Lansing
Robert Lynd
Robert Michael Ballantyne
Robert W. Chambers
Rosa Nouchette Carey
Rudyard Kipling
Saint Augustine
Samuel B. Allison
Samuel Hopkins Adams
Sarah Bernhardt
Sarah C. Hallowell
Selma Lagerlof
Sherwood Anderson
Sigmund Freud
Standish O'Grady
Stanley Weyman
Stella Benson
Stella M. Francis

Stephen Crane
Stewart Edward White
Stijn Streuvels
Swami Abhedananda
Swami Parmananda
T. S. Ackland
T. S. Arthur
The Princess Der Ling
Thomas A. Janvier
Thomas A Kempis
Thomas Anderton
Thomas Bailey Aldrich
Thomas Bulfinch
Thomas De Quincey
Thomas Dixon
Thomas H. Huxley
Thomas Hardy
Thomas More
Thornton W. Burgess
U. S. Grant
Upton Sinclair
Valentine Williams
Various Authors
Vaughan Kester
Victor Appleton
Victor G. Durham
Victoria Cross
Virginia Woolf
Wadsworth Camp
Walter Camp
Walter Scott
Washington Irving
Wilbur Lawton
Wilkie Collins
Willa Cather
Willard F. Baker
William Dean Howells
William le Queux
W. Makepeace Thackeray
William W. Walter
William Shakespeare
Winston Churchill
Yei Theodora Ozaki
Yogi Ramacharaka
Young E. Allison
Zane Grey